# The Shattered Past

I0618902

Janey Clarke

First published in 2025 by Blossom Spring Publishing
The Shattered Past (Devil's Mountain Series)
Copyright © 2025 Janey Clarke
ISBN 978-1-0685693-3-3
E: admin@blossomspringpublishing.com
W: www.blossomspringpublishing.com

# CHAPTER ONE

"Jumping Jehoshaphat! It's a dead body. Stop licking that body, Meg! I've told you not to touch dead things. You daft dog!"

"I'm not dead." He heard his own voice. It seemed to belong to someone else and come from far away. The darkness that he was in had a sliver of light shining above him. Struggling within himself, the light grew brighter, and suddenly it was there all around him. "I'm not dead!"

The slurping noises and the wetness on his cheeks stopped. Doggy breath clung to his nostrils and his eyes blinked open. The brightness of the sun blinded him, and he moved a hand up to shield the glare from his face. But not before he saw the dog sitting beside him. A mongrel cross -type breed, he surmised. It was staring down at him, its tongue lolling and its huge, dark eyes fixed upon him.

"I'm not dead!" Again, he said it. Not only was it for the figure sitting atop the horse, a dark shadow against the sun, but to reassure himself. The figure dropped down lightly from the horse and walked towards him.

"I can't be dead. You've got freckles and no angel ever had freckles!" The words croaked out through his cracked lips. He stared up at the girl and dog, both looking down at him with concern.

"But you sure look dead, Mister. You're all bloody and lying down here in the dirt." He moved gingerly, but the girl spoke sharply. "Don't you move sudden like, or you'll bleed even more. You're covered in blood!" The freckled face, with its snub nose and large, brown eyes, looked intently at the man. "Can you move your arms?"

"Yes, I think so." He gingerly moved one arm, then

the other, and then tried to sit up.

"Let me help you." The strength of her calloused hand with bitten nails surprised him as it helped him rise to a sitting position. "You'll be needing a drink," and she went to her horse, took the canteen from her saddlebag, and brought it over to him.

He took it from her gratefully and began gulping it, but she grabbed it away from him. "Enough. There's barely enough in there for both of us to reach the ranch. That'll have to do you." She stowed the water carefully away, but her eyes kept flicking back towards him.

He was trying to move slowly, each limb at a time. Conscious of her regard, he looked up at her and spoke. "Seems nothing broken. Everything works and I only have an enormous lump on my head. But there's all this blood!" His shirt, a rough, blue check, was thick with drying blood, almost obscuring its garish pattern.

"That's a real hard knock you got on the side of your head. But why are you lying here? Where's your horse got to? And whose blood is on your shirt?" The girl stood, hands now on her hips, still wary of him.

He brushed the flopping blonde hair back from his forehead. Puzzled, he thought over her remarks. Her questions echoed his own thoughts, and he did not have any answers to give her or himself. His hat was still behind his head, his trousers and boots were well worn and had obviously seen hard work.

"Can you check inside your shirt to see if you're still bleeding?"

He unbuttoned a couple of buttons and felt inside, but shook his head, as he did them up again. "Not my blood, but I reckon I'll have to wear this shirt. No way I can go without it in this sun. I don't think there's anything amiss with me, but for this knock on my head. I'm going to stand up." He tried to rise, but the dizziness made him sit back down.

"If it's not your blood, then whose is it?" Her words hung on the dry, searing heat that enveloped them. They both looked at each other, an uneasy horror creeping over them. The questions were not spoken but arose unbidden in each of their thoughts. Who else had been wounded? Where were they? Did they too lie somewhere amongst the rocks in the heat of the afternoon, injured, dying, or dead?

As he looked at the girl, he realised she was looking at him and seeing a potential killer. Somehow, he knew she had checked him for a gun with her first initial glance at him.

"Who are you? What's your name? Where were you going to?" She asked him, insistent now with her anxious questioning.

As he opened his mouth to reply, his eyes widened in shock, and he just stared at the girl. He struggled to rise to his feet, and, with her helping hand, he now stood beside her, unsteady at first, and still clinging on to the nearby rock. He took a deep breath and shook his head, as if to clear it from the residual giddiness. A mistake. The dizziness floated about his head again.

"I'm Amy Tanner. I live at a ranch with my father and brother, Ben. So who are you, Mister? And where were you going?" Her suspicious blue eyes watched him, and she repeated her questions, intent on getting an answer.

Shaking still, he passed a hand over his head, and then he grimaced as it made contact with his lump. The man now stood beside her, unsteady at first. He'd held on to a nearby rock as he gingerly rose to his feet. His mouth opened, "Pleased to meet you Miss Amy, but I have a problem now. I can't remember." The shock he felt at this nothingness in his brain swept over him.

"You can't remember what?" the girl asked him.

"Anything! I don't remember who I am. I don't know what the heck I'm doing here." He swayed a little, steadying himself against the rock. "Still dizzy."

Amy stared at him, silent whilst she thought. As he watched her, he realised she had made some sort of decision. She walked over to her horse. He wondered what her decision had been. "Best you sit down again. I'll have a look round to see if I can find anyone or anything. Your horse may be close by."

He gestured at his bloodstained shirt. "Should you look around? It could be dangerous. If you help me to the nearest town..." His voice trailed into silence.

Amy had shaken her own head violently, and a contemptuous sneer crossed her face. "Too far, and that sheriff is too scared of his own shadow to come up Devil's Mountain. I'll stay within shouting distance." On her horse now, she looked down at him. "Take what rest you can now. It's a long way back to the ranch, especially in this heat. You need all the energy you can get, because sharing a horse we'll need to spell each other walking!"

He nodded. He knew she was talking sense, and he felt too weak to argue, so he moved further into the deeper shade and settled down with his back against a rock. He watched as she rode off, the dog ranging ahead of her on the lookout. What if she kept going? What if she never returned?

# CHAPTER TWO

Amy looked for tracks. The injured man must have come from somewhere. Slight disturbances on the dusty ground made her believe he'd staggered aimlessly along to where he'd finally fallen, and she had found him.

He was a young man about a couple of years older than her, she thought. Good looking too, despite being covered in all that blood. Somehow, and she didn't know why, he didn't seem to be a drifter. He'd been clean-shaven, and that blonde hair of his was clean. Those eyes of his were the brightest blue she'd ever seen. Most of the drifters she'd known had been dirty and unkempt. There was that accent, though. She couldn't place it. Perhaps he was from the East somewhere. She'd heard that they talked funny over that way. Meg had gone up to him and licked him. Meg was an excellent judge of character. She always backed away and even growled at those men she was suspicious of. No, Meg liked and trusted the man. Amy would not trust him. She was not such a fool. But she'd give him the chance to prove himself.

It was Meg who alerted her. The dog stood sniffing the air, ears pricked up and tail alert. Her horse also seemed to check herself and to sniff the air. Meg turned her head towards a large cactus and ran towards it. Amy followed in that direction and found Meg standing over a dead body. This time, she wasn't licking the body. Amy knew, without a doubt, this man was dead. Without dismounting, she moved her horse closer to the body, calming its nervousness with murmurs, and stared down at the man. She saw in that one glance all that she needed to. The man sprawled as if they had flung him down onto the dirt. There were bullet holes. One in his forehead, and the other in his chest, which had bled profusely. Had this been where the unconscious man had been covered in blood? Was it from this victim? She dismounted. Gritting her teeth and suppressing a shudder, she walked towards him. She knelt down.

"Go on, Amy, you have to do it!" She swept her braids back over her shoulder, took a deep gulp of air, and put her hands into the pockets of his heavily bloodstained jacket.

Nothing! She flung the jacket flap to one side and could see at a glance that his trouser pockets were empty as well. Sitting back on her heels, she stared at the dead man. He was an ugly brute of a man, hair tangled and matted with an unruly beard. Whatever this man had carried in his pockets had gone. Whoever had shot him had emptied his pockets and taken his weapons, possessions, and his horse. There was no knowing who or what he'd been. Amy could see that there had been a few horses milling about. She was no Indian Tracker, but she could easily see the disturbed dirt and the hoofprints of several horses. There was a general direction in which they all seemed to go, and that was away from her and away from the ranch. For the first time on encountering the body, Amy breathed a little easier.

Casting a last look at the dead body before riding off, she said a brief prayer for his soul. She guided her horse in a circle around where the injured man lay, hoping there would be some clue as to what had happened. The faint hope that his horse may be wandering around proved to be futile. Realising that she was wasting time and energy, she turned and retraced her way back.

Riding back towards the injured man, her thoughts were still upon the body of the man she had just found.

Who was he? What had he to do with the man she was now helping? What had happened here? And how had it come to pass that there was one man dead, and another man injured? Amy wished she'd never stopped to help the man, that she had just assumed that he was dead and had ridden on home. But that wouldn't have been the Christian thing to do, and her father had raised both herself and Ben to be Christians. She could hear his voice now, "got to face the Lord someday, so best you do the right thing in the here and now."

Amy's horse stumbled. The rocky ground was uneven and tended to catch out an unwary foot or hoof. There was no doubt her horse was limping. She was favouring her near forefoot. Amy was down from the saddle in a second. Lifting the foot, she gazed down at it. Not serious, but there was no way that she could ride her horse. Taking the reins in her hand, she strode off, leading the horse behind her. This was going to pose a big problem. Not only had she an injured man on her hands, now she had no horse for either of them to ride back to the ranch. The journey back was perilous, even for a rider. Now, facing the increasing heat of the afternoon, it was going to be touch and go if they arrived safely back at the ranch. Only a small canteen of water was between them and death from the burning sun.

Could she make it back to Broken Horseshoe Ranch with an injured man and a lame horse?

# CHAPTER THREE

He watched her leave, the scruffy dog running beside her horse. How old was she? About fifteen, he thought, a strange girl. Didn't say much, but she acted decisively and was neither afraid of blood nor this rough desert- like terrain. Those freckles scattered over her nose made him smile. They had been the first thing that had met his eyes when he came to consciousness. He had seen the freckles and the long brown braids hanging down, almost reaching to his face when he awoke. From what? What had gone before that blow on his head? The roughness of the rock behind his back seemed to be the only certain thing in his life at the moment. Heat shimmered in front of him over the ground with its spindly vegetation struggling for a foothold, and the cactus sentinels that stood tall and straight. Somehow, deep within himself, he knew this was strange to him. It wasn't where he'd come from. But where had he come from? Why was he here? Gingerly, he moved his position against the rock. The dizziness was still there when he moved quickly. That had been some blow on his head. He felt gently over it, an enormous lump, almost as big as an egg, but unbroken and there was no blood.

"How did I get this? Who did this to me? Who the hell am I? What's my name?" He shook his head. Another stupid move, he realised when the dizziness returned. Meg arrived, racing over the ground to sit beside him, and woke him from a light doze. Tongue lolling, she gave him a lick on his hand. "Hi Meg," he patted her clumsily, pleased to remember her name. At last, something he remembered! An overwhelming relief swept through his body as he watched the girl walk towards him. He hadn't doubted that she'd return; well, perhaps just a little. A lifeline. That's what she now seemed to him, in his oasis of nothingness. He noted there was a worried frown upon her face, and that she was leading her horse, which was now limping.

"Found a dead body, shot in the forehead and in the chest. He'd lost lots of blood. Maybe that's where you got it from. Nothing else there. His pockets had been emptied, and his weapons were gone. Forgot to ask you, you got anything in your pockets? Do you remember anything yet? Are you still dizzy?" The questions tumbled out from the girl, but she fell silent and watched as he searched deep within the few pockets he had.

"No, nothing in them. I still can't remember anything at all. I remembered Meg's name, and your name is Amy, but I know nothing of what happened before I met you. Has your horse gone lame? I see you're leading it."

Amy nodded and walked over towards him. "Can you stand? Do you think you can walk?" At his assurance that he could do both, she stood beside him, ready to help him if he fell.

With the help of the tall rock that he'd lent against, he stood slowly and carefully, but grinned as he realised he could move easily and that the giddiness had gone. That doze had helped. "Much better. What will we do now? Where are you going? And will you manage without the horse?" He knew deep within himself that he'd been a man of quick decisions, a man used to travelling alone. A solitary life had been his normal one. How he knew that but couldn't remember his own name was a mystery, a puzzle that he kept trying to solve. Relying upon a young girl for his safety and his very life in this wild country did not sit well with him.

"We'll go to our ranch. Pa and Ezra will know what to do. They will sort out this mess."

He took a step forward, then stopped. "My boot, there is a stone or something in my boot." Leaning against his friendly rock, he pulled his boot off and shook it out. A screwed-up piece of paper fell onto the ground. Standing one-legged as Amy bent down to pick it up, she held it out to him, but he shook his head. "Got my hands full. You read it."

Smoothing the crumpled paper out, she scrunched up her face and read. "It says Josh Barnes. Go to the Broken Horseshoe Ranch." Amy flung her pigtails over her shoulder, and her head lifted from the paper. She thrust it under his nose. "Is that your name? Are you Josh Barnes? And what the hell does it mean that you have to go to the ranch?"

He stared down at the piece of paper, reading it again and again. "Josh Barnes? Can that be my name? I don't know, it doesn't sound familiar. As for the ranch, I've never heard of it. Do you know where it is? Have you heard of it?"

"Of course I've heard of it! That's the name of our ranch. That's where I live!" Amy almost shouted the words at him. Her mixed emotions seemed to overwhelm her, as she stared down at the paper held in quivering hands and then up at the man in front of her. He sensed her anger and puzzlement at this strange note.

He stared at her. "I've never heard of it before. I don't understand it. Why would I be coming to your ranch? What does it mean?" Mounting frustration at his helpless predicament and this new unexpected development made him thump the rock beside him. The pain in his hand jarred his whole body, but somehow it brought him back to the reality he was now facing. A reality of blankness, in a world that encompassed the desert around him and this girl, her horse, and dog. That was all he could hold on to in this horrific situation he found himself in. Only the girl, her horse, and the dog. That was all he had to hold on to, to keep the empty blankness away from swallowing him up.

"Okay Josh, I'll call you that for now, even if it's not your real name. We have to go. I don't want to find myself out in the dark, especially not in these mountains. Now we have to walk because my horse is lame. Come on Meg, time to go home." Amy set off, but she kept a watchful eye on him. She knew he was struggling.

At first, he walked stiffly. Something had obviously hurt his shoulder and his back when he had been knocked unconscious. The girl was shrewd and obviously caring. The way she was looking out for him proved it. His hat had been still slung around his neck when he regained consciousness. Grateful now for its shade, he tilted it to keep the blazing sun away from his face. Their feet kicked the dust up as they walked. The horse, as it limped along, created a miniature dust storm. As they passed by the rocks that littered this land, baking heat seemed to be reflected from them.

"I wonder what I am?" His lips were parched, and he thought longingly of the water the girl had in her bag. But she knew the country, she knew when to give them water to drink. Amy had saved his life, better let her continue with the job.

"What you are?" Her voice was weary now, and he realised this walk was taking it out of her. Normally, she would have ridden over this hard ground and have been much closer to home. "What you are?" She repeated.

"Yes. What am I? Am I a lawman? Perhaps a farmer? A gambler, or perhaps a crook." So interested in this line of thought Josh forgot the dizziness in his head, and the discomfort and pain from his shoulder and back, and he walked with an easier gait.

"You always carried a gun," was the remark from the girl beside him that startled him into standing still.

"Why do you say that? How can you tell?"

"When I first found and woke you, immediately, you reached for it. There's a mark on your trousers where your holster usually hung."

Josh's hand crept down to feel the faint roughness of the material, rubbed by the everyday pressure of his gun. "What if I had been a killer? And actually had gone for a gun if that was there beside me?" Josh said softly, looking at the girl.

"One of two things would have happened. I'd have shot you or Meg would have ripped your throat out. Don't be fooled by her. Pa says she is part coyote."

Josh blinked, then his eyes widened as he stared at the girl. "You'd shoot me!"

A laugh escaped from her, and she too stood still and faced him. "You wouldn't be the first varmint I've shot, and I doubt that you'd have been the last one. My Pa wouldn't let me loose up here if I couldn't take care of myself."

Silently they walked on for a while, sweat dripping from Josh and pooling uncomfortably beneath the blood-soaked shirt he wore. How he hated wearing it. It pleased him it wasn't his blood, that went without saying. Whose ebbing life had soaked into his shirt? Could it have been the man that Amy found? Who had killed that man? And who had been violent enough to kill the man and leave him for dead? Who had left him for dead? The questions chased each other around his brain. Stop it, Josh told himself. He didn't know what had happened and questions that went unanswered did him no good. Would they survive this day for him to find out the answers?

# CHAPTER FOUR

"There it is! Up ahead, there may be water in a tiny canyon. If we are in luck, there will be shade and water," Amy said.

Josh couldn't see a canyon, but he hoped the girl was right. He hoped the water was there. The thought of it made him lick his cracked lips with anticipation. Unbelievably, Amy vanished. One minute she was leading her horse alongside a small cliff, and then she'd gone. Her hand came out from behind a rock and pulled at his arm. Guided by Amy, he slid between the rocks of the cliff face and through a narrow opening. How had the horse managed it, he wondered to himself.

Josh found himself in a dark, cave-like canyon, and deep in the shade was a small pool. The cliff walls towered threateningly overhead, jagged peaks surrounded them, and the taller distant mountain of unforgiving heights stood sentinel. The dog and the horse were already drinking, the lapping and slurping breaking into the eerie quiet of the canyon. Josh dropped to his knees beside them. Ever since he had woken from his unconscious state, he had been thirsty. The small amount of water that he'd had from Amy had done little to assuage his thirst. Somehow, it had made the longing for water much worse. They all sat back in the shade; thirst quenched. Water dripped from the dog's muzzle onto the baked earth. The tiredness seeped into Josh's bones from his blow, the blazing sun, and the exercise.

"Come on Josh, time to go. I don't want to be caught up here in these mountains in the dark." Amy refilled the canteen after taking a last drink from the pool. The dog and the horse also drank; seemingly they knew it would be some time before they reached the water again. Josh drank as much as he dared, then rose shakily to his feet and followed her through the narrow, rocky walls out into the blazing sun. Josh felt certain that Meg gave him a sympathetic look and a wag of her tail as they both followed her mistress.

The journey was no longer beside the towering cliffs and rocks of the foothills of the Devil's Mountain. They were going downhill now, and the land seemed to stretch before him, level and endless. A dusty sun-baked land with nothing on it to show the way forward and Josh could see no landmarks. Rock-strewn ground and pebbles underfoot made the unwary step not only painful but hazardous. He turned to look at the girl. "How do you know which way to go?"

"Made it my business to know the land hereabouts when we moved here. Old Ezra showed me the way of it. He's lived his whole life in these parts."

Josh nodded and then thought over her words. "You moved here? Where from?"

A strange look crossed over her face. Amy stopped at once and turned to face him. She pointed at him. "Mister, you must be a newcomer to this land! No one who wants to stay alive asks another person where they come from. It ain't healthy to ask those sorts of questions in these parts."

Startled, Josh stopped and stared back at her. He didn't question what she had said, but it made it obvious to him that perhaps he was a stranger here.

"But," she relented, and continued walking. "But I'll tell you because I got nothing to hide, and you will hear it all from my brother, Ben, anyway. Pa fell ill when Ma died of the fever. Doc told him he needed dry, hot air, and sunshine to get well. He left his job, sold our house, and bought the Broken Horseshoe Ranch. His health has improved, but he's got a load more work and worries. Ben, my young brother, helps around the ranch and he's clever with words. The schooling he needs costs money and is back in the city we came from."

They trudged along in silence. The heat of the day was lessening slightly, as clouds rolled in and the sun moved ever forward to the horizon. She paused for a while. Slipping her hat from her head, she shielded her eyes and stared in front of them. With a sigh, she passed the canteen to Josh, and they took a few sips each. Then she urged the lame horse and Josh on again.

"Look out!" To his surprise, he realised that he'd been trudging along mindlessly, almost dozing. The gunshot shattered the surrounding silence, echoing from the rocky canyon walls and surrounding mountains. Automatically, he had jumped backwards at her shout. Now he stared down at his foot. A snake's head lay there, the body a distance away. If he hadn't turned quickly towards Amy, he would have missed the speed with which she had shot the snake and replaced the gun in her holster. She pulled the loose-fitting canvas jacket she wore over the gun.

"You killed that snake so fast! I didn't know you had a gun under your jacket." His words erupted from him. Relief and shock and astonishment were the emotions that swirled about his brain. That girl could shoot! He'd never seen the movements of the snake, but Amy had not only seen the snake, but she'd also acted at an incredible speed.

"Told you. Need to take care of myself up here." She passed the water bottle to him. This time, he only took a swallow before passing it back to her. He now understood the need to conserve water. Amy's anxious look at the sky made him aware of her eagerness to move faster before nightfall. For someone who wasn't frightened of much, she wasn't keen to spend the night out here. He wondered why, but thought perhaps it would be better if he didn't know. Anyway, he was so exhausted now – he had no breath to spare for conversation. He put one foot in front of the other. His gaze and his thoughts narrowed down to where the next foot should be placed.

Amy strode ahead of him, leading her horse. Occasional checks on its leg were the only stops she now made. Those two brown braids swung down her back, tied at their base with twine. Not a ribbon, not like the other girls would have worn. Her feet were encased in small men's boots, the shape of the square toes evident to his eyes. The skirt of coarse cotton she wore was shorter than normal, not ankle-length. But it made sense, considering the rough ground she was walking upon. It swung from side to side. Somehow, a useless piece of information came into his mind. They placed small metal bars or even shot in the hems for pioneer women. It kept the skirt from blowing in the desert and prairie winds.

Where had that come from? An image of someone who would have been placing them in a hem? Who could that have been? Mother? Sister? That image was fragmented, almost as if it had been a faded sepia print in his mind. Then it was gone. Amy's gun had been in a holster under the men's canvas jacket she wore. He never realised that she even had a gun, let alone that she could use it in that way. Hidden under that jacket, no one could see it. Cool enough, despite the heat of the sun, the jacket kept the worst of the dust from her shirt and skirt and kept the gun out of sight.

"Any help for your father on the ranch?" He ventured as they stopped again for a drink and, this time, they rested in the shade of another huge rock.

"Yes, we have Ezra and Leah. They lived on the ranch when we arrived. It was their home for years, but the owner of the ranch sold it. Ezra and Leah didn't want to move, so we asked them to stay, and we've been grateful for their help and knowledge of the land and property. It's an unforgiving land. To be honest, we would never have survived these months without them. Ezra is an old man now, but his wealth of knowledge about this area helped us settle. When we arrived, he thought we would sack him because of his age, but he'll always have a home with us." Amy got to her feet, brushing the dust from her skirt. "How are you feeling now? You've done well keeping up with me. At this rate, we should get there before dark."

"I'm doing fine," he assured her. It was far from the truth. His head was pounding, and his vision was blurring at times. Had he fallen from his horse? Or been in a fight? His right shoulder and back were painful with every step he took. To stop himself from dwelling upon his aches and pains, he spoke again. "What's the real reason you don't want to be out here in the dark?"

# CHAPTER FIVE

At first, she didn't answer, and he thought she was going to ignore his question. "Bad things happen out here at night." There was a finality in her voice that made it clear she wanted no more questions. They walked on in silence, but curiosity was gnawing away at Josh. He couldn't help himself. He knew she didn't want to say more, but he was curious about her fear, and this place was too eerie for him to let the topic slide. "What things?" Josh asked her.

"Indian massacres, for one. They say this land belongs to the Thunder God. He becomes angry when anyone takes from his land. Folks disappear and are found with their heads missing. Don't want that to happen to me."

"Takes? Takes what?"

"Gold, precious metals," was the stilted reply from her averted face.

"What? Is this gold country?"

"Gold has been found, but the mines have been lost in times past. Few get out alive from the Devil's Mountain if they stay after dark." Her last words were said with such finality that he realised she would add no more to the story.

Shadows were forming. The huge cacti threw long fingers of darkness across their path. The hills changed colour, the rocks showing the deep crevasses and caves in their tawny cliff faces with purple and blue gashes of dark shadow. The towering cliffs where she had found him were behind them now. They cast a looming, eerie presence still, and Josh shivered involuntarily when he turned to look back at them.

"Take care where you are walking. Evening is when

the insects and biting critters appear," she warned.

Would this journey never end? He knew it was becoming a major struggle for his body to keep up with Amy now. The increasingly concerned looks from the girl meant that she, too, realised his growing weakness. One foot in front of another, again and again, took an ever-increasing effort. Each footstep was vital for his life, and he knew he had to keep on moving. Josh almost cannoned into the girl when she stopped suddenly, shielding her eyes against the low setting sun. Josh stared in the same direction. A figure was riding towards them. To his addled gaze, it seemed the figure was swimming through a misty lake when he approached.

"Ezra!" The girl's sudden shout of joy and relief made Josh jump.

A hat was taken from the approaching rider's head and waved frantically.

They placed Josh, despite his protests, on Ezra's horse. He slumped across the saddle and the horse's neck. He knew he was gradually losing consciousness. Aware only of the jolting motion of the horse beneath him, and the voices of the two walking beside him, he drifted into darkness.

"Where did you find him?" Her father stood looking down at the man on the bed that he and Ezra had carried in. Ezra had volunteered to take off Josh's boots and the blood-soaked shirt and to wash the man to remove the bloodstains and dirt.

"I found him near the large group of rocks, and the tall, marked cactus," Amy replied.

She left the bedroom and went to the stove where she lifted the pot and poured herself coffee. Slowly, she sipped the hot brew. Inhaling its aroma, she felt it strengthen her and energise her despite the fatigue she suffered from the long walk. She took the coffee mug and placed it on the kitchen table. Bending down, she reached for the bag that she had dropped on the floor as she'd entered the door. Placing the bag on the table, she began undoing its straps.

Her father came out from the bedroom and also reached for the coffeepot. He poured himself a cup and turned to look at his daughter. He was a big man, or had been before the illness had wasted his body until he was but a shell of that man. An active man: his brown hair and brown eyes had been inherited by both son and daughter. Now, the muscles were withering, and he had a stoop when he walked. The life they had left behind them had been comfortable: a routine established over many years and into which they had all fitted easily. First, his wife had died, leaving an unfillable gap in his life and those of his children. Then he had become ill, and unable to work. His doctor suggested a dry climate would restore his health.

"I don't like you being out there on your own. You could have met those villains that left him for dead and shot the other man. It's not safe on the Devil's Mountain, not for any man and especially not for a young girl like yourself. There's no need for you to go. We'll get by somehow. We'll manage on the ranch, especially if we have some good crops to see us through the coming winter. This continual searching for Jesuit gold is useless. This mountain is called the Devil's own for a reason! There's evil there. It lingers around the mountain. No one comes back. You're risking your life and your sanity going there. Amy, I wish you would stop all this searching." He joined her at the table, sitting down beside her and placing his scalding hot coffee in front of him.

"I'm fine Pa, usually there's nobody around. It's unusual to meet up with folk where I go," Amy replied.

"What was that man doing out there? Left alone, you say, and there was a dead man further back towards the hills." Again, he shook his head and looked towards the bedroom door. The bedroom door opened and Ezra, the old man, came out, carrying a basin of bloodied water and the stained shirt.

"Find out anything, Ezra?" Luke asked him.

"Yes. He's had either a nasty fall on his back, or someone beat him up from behind. I think he fell on top of the murdered man Amy told us about. Sounds as if the dead man bled out and our guy fell on him. He'll be fine. Wouldn't have survived without you coming along, Miss Amy. Sure was his lucky day when you passed by."

"Let's hope that it won't be an unlucky day for us!" Her father said as he walked out the door to check on the horses that Ben was settling down in the dilapidated lean-to they grandly called "the stables".

"Pa, don't you want to see what I found?" Amy called to his retreating back.

"You actually found something? Never thought you would. I thought the map was a fake. Well, girl, what was it you found?"

# CHAPTER SIX

Amy reached into the open canvas bag on the table. She pulled out a small stone. It was polished and had ancient carvings worked on it.

Both her father and Ezra stared down at it. "What is it?" Her father picked it up and turned it over in his hand. It lay on the palm of his hand with the symbols facing upwards, the late afternoon shadows from the window highlighting the carved hieroglyphs. "Amy, what you have found shows that there is something out there. I've seen nothing like this before. Have you, Ezra? Do you understand these symbols?"

"It's a rune, a sacred stone, but not from the Indian peoples. Maybe from far away in time. It could be those people they say came up here, fleeing from the Spaniards." Ezra fingered it, his jagged, bitten nail tracing the strange symbols on it. "There is the remote possibility of it being from the Jesuits. If it was a link to the ancient Jesuits' trails, that could mean the map is true after all."

"Funny you should say that, Ezra." Amy flicked her braids back over her shoulder, looked at both men from one to the other, and gave a triumphant grin as she pulled out of the bag a coin. "It's a Spanish coin, isn't it?"

The two men looked down at the coin lying in her hand. Her father took it from her and held it up to the light, then passed it over to Ezra. "It's Spanish, definitely a Spanish coin. Can you remember where you found it? Do you think there's any chance of any more there? Was it buried? How did you find it?" The words tumbled out of Luke, as he handed it over to the grizzled old man.

"I had that old map memorised. The one you gave me,

Ezra, the one the old Mexican gave you saying it was a map of the Jesuits trail. There was a symbol marked on it, and another one in line with it on one of the large rocks. I found the symbols, but to my surprise, the symbols were not on a rock but carved on a large cactus. It towered above me. It must have been really old. This tiny pebbly stone with the markings on it was lying beneath it, and I pottered around it and found the coin."

Ezra, whilst Amy had been talking, turned the coin over and over in his hands. He even lifted it up to his mouth and gave a tiny nip to the coin with his remaining two teeth. He nodded his head, the white hair falling forward as he did so. "It's genuine. I reckon Spanish as well. The story goes that there were two hundred odd mules carrying the gold; stands to reason some coins would have fallen along the way. Don't get your hopes up Amy, this may just be a lucky find. But it's worth taking another look. I reckon I'll come with you next time, knowing the land as I do. Together, we may really get lucky!" Ezra rarely smiled, but he did just then. The wrinkled face creased open wide into a gummy grin. "Yes, we may get lucky!"

Amy's father's face grew solemn, and he looked at them both. "This must be hidden. Say nothing to Ben. Nor the stranger. Ben chatters about everything and the least said about these finds the better. Well done, Amy, you did good today. But I still don't like you out there alone. Finding the wounded guy, and a dead man, proves that there are others out there. What do you think they were after, Ezra?" Whilst he had been speaking, Luke had wrapped the coin and the stone in a cloth. Walking over to the shelves on the wall, he pressed a slight knot on the wooden backing. A panel slid to the side and a small aperture was revealed. Dropping the cloth parcel beside other parcels and a couple of small boxes, he slipped the panel back into place. "Good hiding place this is, Ezra. Clever trick you made!"

"Could you understand those markings on the stone, Ezra?" Amy asked the old man again. She picked up the coffee mug and drank the coffee down to the dregs.

"No, I've seen nothing like that before," was his reply.

"Would any Indian understand it?" Amy pressed the old man.

Slowly he shook his head, the white hair moving as he did so. He stroked his beard, which was now white, whilst his faded blue eyes looked at the girl. An old man, he had feared that the new owners would turn him and his wife out of their home when the previous owner had died suddenly in his bed. The rancher's son, living in the big city, wanted no more to do with the ranch. He'd hated it when he'd grown up there and couldn't wait to be rid of it. Luke, desperate for a new start in a place his doctor deemed suitable for his health, had jumped at the low price. The price that had been suggested had suited his budget. The rancher's son agreed to tie up the deal quickly. No one had given any thought to Ezra and his wife, Leah.

It was with astonishment that Luke, Amy, and Ben had arrived with their possessions to find the couple living in a log cabin behind the main ranch house. The elderly couple, fearing the worst, had their belongings ready and packed. Luke, however, realising the difficulties this new life would have, and how little he knew of ranching and this area, jumped at the chance of having help. Ezra and Leah unpacked their belongings, and it wasn't long before mutual friendliness grew up between both families. The gratitude from Ezra and Leah was rewarded by their easing the city family into the difficulties and hardships of ranching life. To show how grateful they were, Ezra had produced a map of the surrounding hills. It was a treasure map that a dying Mexican he had helped had given him. The Mexican told him it showed the trail that the Jesuits had taken with their gold when they fled into the hills. It showed the trail in a locality near to the ranch, going up into the Devil's Mountain. The Mexican said this map showed the way to an actual location of the treasure. Along the trail, when the mules had died, the gold from each mule had been buried and symbols were placed around the caches of gold.

"If we find some of the gold, it will mean Ben can go to college and you, Pa, can have that specialist treatment doctors said would benefit you." The two men nodded at the enthusiastic young girl, but they looked at each other, knowing how remote the possibility of Amy finding the treasure would be. Or would it? Had she already taken the first step with the ancient map to finding the gold?

# CHAPTER SEVEN

"Finding that coin may mean that the map is correct after all." Her father looked at Amy. "You have to be careful. I know I keep saying that, but I don't like you going there alone. Finding this injured man shows what's going on out there. There are others seeking gold and looking for lost mines."

"But I'm not looking for a goldmine! Where I search is far away from where the maps show the mines to be. This is just a chance encounter. No one goes on the trails I use. I reckon they lost their way," Amy said.

"What about the sheriff? Should I ride into town to tell him about the dead man and that wounded fellow?" Ezra said.

Before Luke could reply, they heard shouts from Ben. "There's a rider coming! Look, in the distance, there's a rider coming." The door was flung open and Ben rushed in. Amy looked at her brother. The excitement in his face was obvious. Her arrival, accompanied by the injured man, was an unusual experience and had made a welcome change in the boy's humdrum life. Thirteen years old, Ben had been forced to grow up prematurely. It worried Amy that her brother grew up starved of company. His hair, a light brown, similar to hers and their father's, stood up in peaks where Ezra had cut it short amidst an onslaught of Ben's complaints. This haircut, added to his many freckles and the grin that he mostly wore, made him look so much younger than his thirteen years. Their mother's death with the fever had been sudden, and their father falling ill with it shortly afterwards had been terrifying for both of them. Their father's gradual recovery had left him with a weakness that meant he could not resume his previous occupation. It had been an advert in a newspaper that had sent them across the vast country of America to arrive at this ranch in the foothills of the Devil's Mountain. Aware that no regular income could be got because his health was so precarious, and acting on his doctor's advice, their father purchased the Broken Horseshoe Ranch. It had eaten up most of their savings. The journey, which was both long and difficult, had left her father considerably weakened, and left them little money to live on.

On their arrival, Amy had felt that the decision to leave the city that they had lived in had been a mistake. The ranch itself was rundown and in poor condition. There was no stock and no income to be wrung from the failing ranch. The old man that had previously lived there could not look after the place properly, partly because he was old and partly because he was too mean to spend any money on it. His son, enjoying life in San Francisco, refused to return and gladly accepted any offer on the property.

Amy's naïve father had got the ranch for a good price but had been horrified to see the state of it, and the isolation of it from the nearest town. On their arrival, they had found the elderly foreman and his wife ready with their possessions packed in the log cabin they had called home for many years. They had been told of the sale, and that the new owners would not necessarily want them to work on the ranch. It had been with Ezra's help that Amy had put her ailing father to bed on their arrival. Ezra had helped Amy find out how to establish a routine for living on the ranch. Without their help, it is doubtful that the family would have survived. Their presence in the log cabin had made Amy's life easier and, for that alone, they could stay as long as they wished.

"Someone's coming. There's a rider coming from town. I think it's the sheriff," Ben repeated.

They all walked to the porch and stood watching. The rider in the distance was getting closer. Amy could see that Ben had been correct. It was the sheriff. There was no mistaking that heavy horse and the even heavier rider who sat upon it. Sheriff Cody was an enormous man. They had elected him sheriff because no one else wanted the job. The small town was just a collection of tents, hastily built dwellings, and a few commercial enterprises owned by hopefuls waiting for the town to grow. So far, it hadn't.

"Well, Sheriff. Not often we see you out here." Amy's father stepped forward to welcome the man as he dismounted from his horse. Ben ran forward to take the horse, leading it to the stable. Amy smiled to herself as she watched Ben take his time, eager to hear why the sheriff had come out to the ranch.

Why had the sheriff come? The lazy man sat all day in the office, his booted feet stretched out on his desk. Apart from that, his time was spent in the saloon, drinking and chatting with the most disreputable inhabitants of the town of Nowhere. Amy eyed the man with suspicion. The stories she'd been told by Ezra concerning this man made her wary. It was said that he did nothing without an ulterior motive. His greed for food, drink, and women was legendary. Why had the sheriff arrived at their ranch? What was he planning for them?

# CHAPTER EIGHT

Josh woke to the sound of voices. Bewildered, he raised himself upon his elbow on the worn sheets and patchwork quilt that lay on the old-fashioned, metal frame bed and glanced around. He was in a small room. The split logs around the walls had a variety of wooden pegs on which hung some men's clothes. A shelf held some books and a photo frame. A couple on their wedding day stood self-consciously, he in his best suit, she clutching a small bunch of flowers. They looked young and the clothes they wore were old in style, so it had been taken some time ago. A small window had a thin hide across the opening. Light slid beneath it into the darkness of the room. Judging by the angle of the sun's rays, it was late afternoon. He was conscious of the driving pain in his head, and every movement jarred his back and arm.

"The girl Amy. And Meg the dog." His voice was only a whisper in the room, but he felt it reverberate in his own head. It was the only memory he had. That realisation struck him with a force that almost winded him. It was the only memory he had! Moving slowly, anxious not to set off the pounding headache that he remembered from the walk, he swung his legs over the edge of the bed, placing his feet on the floor. Looking down at his own body, he realised that he still had his trousers on, but he was wearing a new, clean shirt. Shuddering, he remembered the bloodstained shirt he had worn on that journey to this... "Where am I? What am I doing here?" Again, his whisper seemed to echo around the room. That girl with the plaits and freckles, she found him and brought him here. No! It was the dog who found him. He remembered the doggy smell and the rasping licks of her tongue. The dog's face with the dark patch over one eye had made him smile then, and it did now. He liked Meg!

Loud voices had woken him. They were in the next room. Josh rose to his feet and walked towards the doorway, listening intently. The first voice he heard was noisy and somehow aggressive.

"I rode to the Grangers over the hill to warn them, and then I came on to you folks. I got to tell you there is a gang of bank robbers roaming these hills. Be on the lookout and keep close to home. Just like to make sure everyone gets told about these things. Just doing my job as a sheriff!" The man gave a hearty guffaw. There was a silence in the room.

Josh was paralysed with indecision. Was he a bank robber? Had he killed somebody? What did the others think out there? He'd been unconscious, out of it, when they brought him in. Josh only vaguely remembered voices around him as he'd been helped down off the horse. Thinking back, he remembered an old guy took the bloodstained shirt off him and washed him down, easing him into the shirt that he now wore. Did they think he was a bank robber? Were they going to burst into the room and haul him off to jail? Josh looked at the tiny window. Should he attempt to leave? That was a fool's game! No way would he survive out there on his own. He drew closer to the door, listening hard through a gap in the logs.

"Thank you kindly, Sheriff. We appreciate you coming by and warning us. Shows us all what a good heart you have, and how you are looking after us. Yes, Sheriff, we really appreciate it."

Josh didn't know who was speaking, but he faintly recognised the voice as that of the man who had greeted Amy upon their arrival. He detected a faint touch of hypocrisy in the man's words. Would the sheriff have the wit to realise that?

The man continued speaking. "We've been working round the ranch today. Getting on with the chores as usual. No strangers, nothing out of the ordinary today. But we'll be on the lookout now. Don't want to tangle with bank robbers. So thank you kindly, Sheriff. Appreciate it."

"Well, folks, I'll be on my way, going to call in on the Widow Perkins on my way back to town. That'll be my last visit for the day."

Josh stayed where he was, listening as the footsteps went out onto the porch. He heard the sheriff ride away. Indecision swept through him. It was a strange feeling, a new feeling. He knew he'd never been a man that couldn't make up his mind, a man that dithered. No, he knew deep within him he had been a man who had decided on a course of action and then acted upon it. What the hell had happened to him?

"Pa, why didn't you tell the sheriff about the man in the bedroom?" A boyish voice. That must be Ben, Amy's younger brother, Josh thought.

"Don't think he could be a villain, otherwise he'd have ridden off with the gang. They left him for dead, stripped him of his gun and everything he had with him. I think he was innocent of the bank robbing and somehow got caught up with them. That sheriff is a lazy fool. He'd have taken him off to jail and called him a bank robber."

"But Pa, why would he do that?" Ben asked his father.

"Because that sheriff wants to be re-elected. He's bone

idle, but capturing a bank robber would prove he wasn't as bad as we all know he is. It wouldn't matter if Josh was innocent or not. The sheriff would let him go to trial. Then, if he was innocent, it wasn't the sheriff's fault. He was just doing his duty," was the reply.

"By that time, the sheriff would have been re-elected," Amy said in disgust.

"If he isn't a bank robber, then who is he? And what was he doing out here?" Ben asked.

Josh had heard enough. Amy had saved his life. Now her family had saved him from going to jail. Josh stood up. For a moment, his head swam a little, and he thought he'd fall. Thankfully, the giddiness cleared, and he felt better. Straightening the borrowed shirt, he walked over to the door. For some reason, he was nervous about meeting these people. It shouldn't be difficult, but it was! He realised that going into a room with people that were unknown to him, apart from the girl, had become a major difficulty. Why? He'd never been nervous before, or had he? That was it. He couldn't remember, couldn't remember anything. That left him feeling at a disadvantage, as if he was unarmed or unclothed.

"Come on Josh, pull yourself together, man." That was another problem. His name wasn't Josh. He knew it was not Josh. How he knew that was a puzzle to him. But until he could remember, Josh it would have to be.

The door gave a loud creak as he walked into the main room of the ranch. In the corner was a pot-bellied stove, the pipe leading up out of the roof. A coffeepot sat on it, the aroma filling the room. There were shelves at the side of it, the collection of jars and packets showing it was the store cupboard. In the middle of the room stood a large table, with three roughly made chairs around it. A bench sat under the window, which was a square cut out of the log wall, covered by a thin, scraped hide. A piece of canvas hung beside it, ready for night-time draughts.

Every person in the room turned at the noise of the creaking door to stare at Josh. The girl – Amy – yes, that was her name. A small glow of pride burned within him at his feat of memory. A young boy sat beside her on the bench beneath the window. The same freckles were splashed on his nose, and his long, floppy hair was a similar shade of nut brown to his sister's. The broad grin that creased his face at the sight of Josh made him smile.

A tall man stood by the stove. He was an older version of the man in the photograph. Once a powerful man, he was now a gaunt shell of what he had once been. But the brown eyes shone with intelligence and determination despite the frailty of his body. The last person in the room sat on a chair, his elbows on the table, a tin mug clasped in his hands. White hair hung down almost to his shoulders, and the white beard was long and straggly. He looked Josh up and down with a calculating stare. Josh felt uneasy. He was uncertain what this man was thinking and how he would react to his presence here. Perhaps he would have been better off going with the lazy sheriff after all!

"Reckon you're feeling better now. You'll take a mug of coffee?" The tall man by the stove reached for the pot that was sitting on the stove and poured a mug of the scalding brew. He gestured for Josh to sit at the table.

"I've got to thank you folks. I heard what you told the sheriff. Thanks." Josh took a sip of the brew. It was strong and, to his astonishment, it was real coffee. Not some adulterated mix using dandelion or roasted wheat. This was the real thing, and he felt it put a new life in him as the scalding brew slid down his throat. "This is excellent coffee!" Was all he could say.

"We may have come out here into the wilds, but the one thing I can't give up, and I won't, is my coffee," Luke said and sat down beside Josh. "You've met my daughter, Amy. I'm Luke Tanner, and this is my ranch. Over there is my son, Ben, and this is Ezra who met with you on the trail."

"Thank you, you've been very kind to me." Josh sat down on the chair, surprised at how weak he felt even just walking from the bedroom. He sank down onto it with a sigh of relief that was not unnoticed by the others.

"Takes a bit of getting over, does a knock on the head," Ezra said with a sympathetic smile.

Josh drank the coffee gratefully. The aroma from the steam alone seemed to give him a new life, and he drank it appreciatively. He put the mug down on the table in front of him. Taking a deep breath, he looked at Luke and said, "I heard it all. I think the voice of the sheriff woke me up. I don't remember being put to bed." Josh fingered the clean shirt. "Thanks for the clean shirt. I don't even remember the other one coming off. Thanks." Lifting the coffee mug again, he was about to drink the very last dregs, but Luke, sitting nearest to the stove, lifted the pot up and refilled his mug. "Thanks, thanks again for everything." Josh took another large drink of the coffee, swallowed it down, and placed the mug on the table. "Why did you lie to the sheriff about me?"

# CHAPTER NINE

All eyes turned to Luke. "We only arrived here some months ago, but from what I've learnt from Ezra and a few folks friendly towards us, that sheriff is a man to be wary of. Eager to put anyone in his jail because it makes him look good. Then they get shipped off for trial to the next town. A good few have been innocent. Some that were guilty got lost on their journey, if you know what I mean. Seemed to me those villains left you for dead, stripped you of all your belongings. Didn't seem like you were with the villains. I felt sure that you were a victim. That's what I reckon, Josh Barnes."

Luke picked up the piece of paper that had been screwed up in the toe of Josh's boot, smoothed it out, and glanced at him. "This piece of paper is a real puzzle. Until you get your memory back, or we find out what this message means, I reckon, Josh Barnes, that you are my nephew, newly arrived from way out East. That should take care of your visit and your accent. You've come to give your poor uncle a hand as he settles out here in the wild West."

Ezra smiled, that gummy grin of his was wide. "That be good! A real good story, Luke. What do you think, Josh Barnes? You happy with that as well?" The old man looked at him, and that toothless grin grew wider at the expression on Josh's face. There was bewilderment at first as he struggled to take in the story that Luke had made up to explain his presence at the Broken Horseshoe Ranch. Then Josh nodded. "Yes, that's a good story. I'm pleased to visit with you, Uncle Luke, and to meet my cousins, Ben and Amy. Reckon I'll enjoy my visit."

Laughter erupted in the room at his words.

"I always wanted a brother, but a cousin will do me just fine!" Ben said.

"There's just one thing that worries me in this made-up story," Josh said thoughtfully as he drained his second mug of coffee. "What happens when I recover my memory? What happens then?"

There was silence, and then Luke spoke. "We'll cross that bridge when we come to it."

Ezra rose to his feet. "I'll finish the chores outside and get to my bed. See you in the morning, young fella." Ezra gave Josh a pat on his back as he walked past him to the door. He gave a nod to Luke and was gone.

"I'll get our meal," Ben said, jumping to his feet and dashing out after Ezra.

"Ezra and Leah live in a small cabin behind ours. They lived here for many years, and we've been glad of their help to settle in. Ezra helps with the chores, and Leah cooks us an evening meal. Ben is going to get it and tell Leah all about you," Luke explained.

Josh watched Amy as she got up from the bench and began readying the table for the meal. There wasn't much to do. They had a knife and fork for everyone, mismatched. The coffee mugs were cleaned out and filled with water. That was it. Josh got a glimpse, a tiny memory glimpse, of a table laden with gleaming cutlery, white napkins, and crystal glasses. There had been voices and laughter, pretty dresses on beautiful women, and elegantly dressed men. It was gone. Where had that come from?

"How much conversation did you hear?" Amy asked him, standing across the table and staring at him, searching for any glimpse of what he was thinking on his face. "Was it only the conversation when the sheriff came?"

"Yes, that was when I was fully awake. I heard murmuring voices before that, but I don't remember what they said. I don't think I was properly awake then," was his reply.

The door opened, and Ben came in, carrying a large, heavy pot. An older woman followed him. Josh realised this must be Leah. She followed Ben, carrying a tin plate piled high with sourdough rolls. Josh had known he was thirsty, but hadn't realised how hungry he was. He found it hard to stop salivating as he glanced at the rolls, and the smell of the stew reached his nostrils.

"When I get the blood out of that shirt, you'll get it back," was her first remark to Josh. Do married couples get to look like their partners after many years, or was that likeness already present when they got married? Josh wondered as he watched Leah place the food on the table. Smaller in stature, but Leah had the same long white hair and almost the same expression as her husband. Thank goodness she hadn't got his beard, was the ridiculous thought that crossed Josh's mind. "Thank you, Leah. I'm sorry to put you to so much trouble with that shirt."

Leah stared at him. "Ezra was right, that's a strange way you have of talking." Her eyes raked him up and down. She turned to Luke, nodded her head. "He'll do." Leah turned on her heel and walked out of the door.

"That's Leah for you!" Amy laughed at his expression. "She's been amazing to us, does all the cooking and laundry. In return, they live here."

Nothing was said for some time. Ben had rushed in, shaking his hands free from drops of water, and showing them to his sister as he sat down at the table. She nodded and gave him a dish of stew. Josh watched this byplay between brother and sister, realising Ben had been under instructions to wash his hands before his meal. Interest in them waned as he ate the meal, relishing every mouthful.

"When did you last eat? You are famished, aren't you?" Ben said through a mouthful of stew.

"I'm hungry, starving. So it must have been some time ago. Will I ever remember?" His last words escaped him, his frustration now mingled with anger. What had happened to him?

Luke placed his fork carefully on his plate. He stared across the table at Josh. "Fate has dealt you this hand. You have two choices, Josh. Get angry, frustrated, and constantly try to remember. That's useless. Your memory will return when it returns, not before. The other choice you have facing you is acceptance. You're safe and warm and well fed. Just be thankful to God for His deliverance of you, and don't push yourself into that pit of despair. It's easy enough to fall into it. God willing, we can all hope and pray for the future calmly."

"Yes Luke. I am grateful to Amy and all of you. I am frustrated and angry. You got me there! But I feel so useless. I feel there should be something that I need to do, somewhere I should be. That's what's getting me so..." His voice faded away as he tried hard to explain himself. A glance at the older man made him feel ashamed. This man was seeking to help him, trying to bring acceptance into his mind to ease his angry frustration. Luke was facing death, and he had suffered the loss of his wife, career, and home. The journey here to this desolate place must have been hell for him, frail and weak as he was. Yet here he was sympathising and trying to ease Josh's burden. Josh felt small. "Thank you, Luke."

"Ben has his schoolwork. He does that every night.

He's a bright lad, should really go on to a college back East. I settle down with a book or the Bible, and Amy does her mending and such like," Luke told him as he rose to his feet and went over to the small shelves placed haphazardly on the wall. "I couldn't come all this way without some books! Books and coffee! That's all I need." Luke gave Josh a smile as he pulled the books down from the shelf.

"Can you read, Josh? Did you go to school?" Ben asked as he placed his books on the table in the light from the oil lamp that he had placed in its centre. Then he looked at Josh and laughed. "I expect you can't remember. Here, see what you make of this."

# CHAPTER TEN

Ben pushed the book towards Josh who lent over it, looking down carefully at the words in front of him. He recognised it at once. "Why, it's that Mark Twain book. I've read it! I read it and..." The memory wouldn't come. Yes, he'd read it, but when and where eluded him. "So what are you doing then with this book? It's a splendid book. I enjoyed it."

"I write the words out and then practice them again and again. Then I write some of my own words."

Ben's writing was still childish and carefully formed, as if by someone who does not write frequently enough to find it easy. It surprised Josh to see how much the boy had written. There were pages and pages of it. When he had run out of paper, Ben had used the backs of packets, and even the inside of feed sacks. Ben's enthusiasm for the work was clear in his writing.

"Ben should go to college. He needs the proper tuition and the materials to further his education," Amy said. Her glance at her brother held pride and affection, but Josh realised she ached to do more to further his career. Without even a word, Josh understood Amy didn't want her young brother to grow up on a half derelict ranch and end his days unfulfilled.

"I don't want to go away from here. I love the life here on Broken Horseshoe Ranch. I didn't like the school I went to. They made me do things like algebra and Latin. That was no use to me! All I want to do is write and live my life here. Don't worry about me, Sis, I shall do fine living here. I would have thought that you'd miss city life, all the parties and dances that you no longer attend. Don't you miss dressing up in fine clothes, Amy?"

Ben was teasing his sister, but Josh saw in the boy a maturity which far outstripped his years. From looking at Ben, Josh turned to face Amy. What was her reaction to the remarks of Ben going to be? Surely, the young girl would long for pretty clothes, dances, and music, and the companionship of other young women?

"No, Ben, I hated dressing up and going out to those awful parties. I was always tearing my skirt or dropping some food or spilling a drink. I could never cope with the other girls and their nasty remarks. They could be so spiteful, I'd far rather tackle a rattlesnake than some of those mean girls I met!" Amy replied vehemently to Ben.

"Surely not a rattlesnake? They can't have been that bad, can they?" Josh laughed at the indignant expression on the girl's face.

"You didn't have freckles! And long, straight, ordinary brown hair! Those two things, along with my height, made me a target for all the nasty, spiteful remarks they could think of!" Amy spat the words out.

Both Ben and Josh laughed. They couldn't help it. After a moment, Amy joined in the laughter. Then she rose to her feet. "Come on, Ben, time for bed for all of us."

Josh stood up. The bed he had slept in earlier had obviously been Luke's bedroom. The sick man had gone in, closing the door firmly behind him after his "good night" to them all. What now? Where was he to sleep? "Do I go out to a barn or something?" He asked them, feeling awkward.

"No, Josh, I have a small room to myself. Ben opens out these rugs and mattresses and sleeps in here. There is plenty for you to join him," Amy replied.

"It's the best spot in the house, nice and warm and

cosy," said Ben. He took the pile of rugs and patchwork quilts and pulled out from underneath them a couple of mattresses. The ticking covers on both of them were freshly laundered, Josh noticed, and they were filled with feathers.

"They are very comfortable, and the rugs keep us toasty," Ben said, and laid a mattress on either side of the stove, ready for them. "I'll go outside first. The privy is just behind the cabin."

Amy came in, shivering. "It's cold out there. Good night, Josh. I hope you sleep well."

On Ben's return, Josh went out of the door and turned right behind the cabin as Ben had told him. The privy was just where Ben had said. Josh noticed it was serviceable and kept clean. But it needed further repairs to the roof and the walls.

He came out and stood for a moment. The moon, which had been halfway in shadow when he went into the privy, had now emerged from behind the clouds. It lit up the ranch and the cabin where Ezra and Leah lived and the surrounding countryside. He took a deep breath. The air was chilly but so fresh it seemed to sparkle into his lungs. They needed repairs wherever he looked. It had been only a few months since they had moved here, so little time. Whoever had owned it before them had had many years in which to let it fall into disrepair. Josh shook his head at the neglect. He began walking back and stood on the porch, looking around. The moon shone with a pitiless glare upon the ranch, highlighting every chore and repair that needed doing. The Devil's Mountain loomed up behind the ranch. Dark and forbidding, even the moonlight could only light up a few faces of the jagged peaks and cliffs. An impenetrable cloak of eerie blackness hid most of it.

Josh gave a last glance at the mountain. It held the secret of who he was and what had happened to him. He knew that instinctively. The answer to his memory loss lay within the mountain. Despite himself, he shuddered at the thought of returning to it. But he knew he had to. Devil's Mountain held the secret of his past, and the key to his future.

Josh stood gazing up at the moon. He put his hand on the rail and thought again, as he had so many times that day, of what had happened to him. What had his life been? Who had he been? No matter how he tried, nothing returned. Only the faintest wisp of a memory seemed to taunt him as it drifted across his mind. His grip tightened on the wooden rail as anger surged within him. When he found out what had happened, and who had left him for dead, he would make them pay. In the cold glare of the moonlight, a thirst for revenge grew cold and deadly within his heart.

# CHAPTER ELEVEN

The following day, Luke was ill in the morning. A worried Amy was staying close to home in case she was needed to help her father. The sun shone as it did nearly every day, but the saving grace of the Broken Horseshoe Ranch was its proximity to a spring. The clear, sparkling water bubbled into a small creek at the back of the ranch. In a land parched and dry from the ever-present sun, it was a rare and valuable asset.

The day passed quickly for Josh. At times, he had to pause because the pain from the injuries in his back and shoulder would grip him painfully. His head ached only a little from the blow he had suffered. But he found that if he were to move too quickly, the dizziness would arise again.

"It's great having your help, Josh," Ben told him quite a few times during the day. The boy talked non-stop throughout their tasks. Josh heard all about their life in the city. Their idyllic life had been cut short after the fever had ravaged the family. Ben missed only one friend. The boy's constant talk had been mostly about his English master. The man had obviously taken pity on the child coping with the drama at home and had encouraged him in his writing.

Josh helped Ben repair the many holes in the cabin's fabric and the privy. The draughts coming through the logs must have been terrible in the winter, Josh thought. In summer, the dust would be blown endlessly through the rooms. There were some walls made of adobe. These had stood against the ravages of fluctuating temperatures and the constant winds.

Leah and Amy worked hard together. Josh could see

them attending to laundry, sweeping out the rooms, and clearing out the henhouse. Josh felt Amy was trapped in a life that she had never been brought up in, but marvelled at the cheerful manner in which she carried out the repetitive, endless daily tasks of the ranch.

"Do you know anything about gardening? Or plants? I'm trying to grow some vegetables, but don't seem to have much luck. Ezra only plants corn. I have a fancy to grow some green vegetables." Luke stood with a spade at the edge of the freshly turned soil. The man was weak and had risen from his sickbed despite the protests from Amy and Leah. He was trying to ready the soil for planting.

"What made you come to this ranch?" Josh asked Luke. "There must have been many other ranches for sale. Why pick this one?" Amy, who had been hanging clothes on the line, stood still and looked around the large shirt she had been pegging out. This conversation she obviously wanted to hear.

"It's where it is, Josh. All my life, I have read stories of people doing exciting and wonderful things. You must think me mad, facing this dreadful disease, with two children, yet I set off to have one last adventure."

"You're looking for goldmines in the hills, aren't you?" Josh said, gazing at the man. There was so much he didn't remember of his own life, but he knew men wagered everything to find gold in the hills. Surely Luke wasn't such a man? An educated man, who surely had more sense than to follow a gold rush. Dredging back into his lost memory, somehow he remembered California had been the centre of the gold rush in '49. Many miners had done well, but they were the ones who had arrived early on the scene. Most of the gold hunters had ended up destitute and broken men.

"There were three choices I could make. I wanted only the properties I could afford, not too far from a town. I needed enough of a spread, giving us the chance to be self-sufficient, to enable us to live off the land. The knowledge that this one had year-round water was a deciding factor. But only this one was near to my dream. No, Josh, I'm not seeking a goldmine. But it is gold I'm after. The story of the Jesuits has fascinated me, taking the gold bars on mules and hiding it." Luke sat on a bench on the porch in the shade and laughed at the expression on Josh's face. The older man's lined face was transformed as he grinned at Josh.

"Jesuits and mules?" Josh thought Luke had been affected badly by his illness, not merely in his lungs but in his brain as well. This he had to hear. He sat down on the top step, turning around to face the man. Josh's long legs spread out, and his back and shoulder gave him only a twinge as he lent back against the porch rail. Pushing his floppy, blonde hair from his eyes, he wondered when he could get it cut. After seeing Ezra's handiwork on Ben, he was going to put up with its length. Out of the corner of his eye, he could see that Amy had ducked under the washing line, and was now pegging the clothes out, facing them. An anxious expression on her face as she listened made him wonder at what Luke was about to reveal.

"The Jesuits had missions; some had become extremely profitable plantations. All the Jesuits were known to be gathering together gold and silver. Some said it was from Aztecs who had previously mined in the south-west of America. Others said that the Jesuits had built mission houses with successful plantations of crops, and always close by a silver and gold mine. They had stored much of their wealth ready to send back to Portugal or Spain, I'm not sure which. News from Europe reached them that the Jesuits were not in favour back home, and many of their brothers were being attacked, so they gathered up the gold and silver and took flight."

"Is this documented? Is it a true story?" Josh thought it sounded unlikely and felt certain that Luke had been bamboozled into making a rash decision to arrive here.

"Some of it's true, some of it may just be fairy tales. I knew someone where we lived before who had a cousin who found a Spanish coin near to here. He would have carried on searching but was bitten by a snake which left him paralysed in one arm. The man was lucky to escape with his life. The story intrigued me and I did some research in the library and checked out some old newspapers. There was much of what he said that I could see was documented in books and in the papers. We had to move, so why not this ranch which was close to his find?"

"So this is what Amy is doing. She's going out searching for the Jesuits' gold?" Josh said to Luke, all the while conscious of Amy drawing near to them and now standing listening openly to their conversation.

"Amy's located some markings on the map that Ezra was given. The story continues with the legend that the Jesuits vacated the missions with two hundred and forty mules laden with gold and silver bars. They were taking it to hide, to enable them to find it later, after they had gone back to Europe. They were fearful of persecution and had the gold ready for their return. That's one version of the story, but I have heard other versions."

"So there are gold and silver bars just lying about from

the two hundred and forty mules? That's quite a treasure. Are there many other treasure seekers out there?" Josh asked Luke.

"Not where we are looking. There are maps showing locations of the mines that the Jesuits used. They are far off round the other side of the mountains. I don't think they would have buried it back there. I'm hoping we have the right map and the right area to search for the Jesuit gold."

Josh did not know what to think about this story. Was there truth in it? Or had Luke been carried away by fanciful tales?

They stopped at midday, but it was only to have some hard biscuits and gravy dished up by Leah. Josh was exhausted. His head was pounding, and the bruises on his back and shoulder seemed to have a life of their own. The essential work to nail the boards in place which they had embarked upon plagued him with intermittent pain. The large woodpile to be used for repairing the damage by storms and the extreme temperatures of the region had diminished. Both he and Ben had worked tirelessly throughout the morning. With the two of them, it had been simple work to nail the boards in place. Josh felt already he was working for his keep. He sat on the steps leading up to the porch.

Luke was working on the project he had embarked upon earlier: a vegetable garden. On a visit to the town of Nowhere, he'd heard of others using their land to plant summer crops, which would not only help them be self-sufficient in the hottest months, but could help them survive through the winter. Luke had no knowledge of any gardening. Struggling in a strange environment with his limited strength was proving an arduous task for the sick man.

"Thank you both. You and Ben have worked hard this morning. Appreciate it," Luke said to Josh. A surreptitious glance sideways by Josh showed the older man ashen-faced and struggling for breath. Out of the corner of his eye, Josh had watched him all morning. Luke had done what he could, trying to plant seeds and watering them into place. But even that had been too much for the sick man.

"Pa, why don't you have a rest? It's the hottest part of the day now. You can work again when it's cool this evening," Amy said to her father, a look of concern on her face.

"Yes, I'll get more done this evening," was his weary reply.

Josh watched the sick man climb the steps to the porch and enter the cabin. He heard the coffeepot being lifted off the stove, and the tin mug being filled with Luke's eternal need for coffee. Then the heavy footsteps and the bedroom door closing on Luke.

What would happen if Luke died? How would it affect Ben and Amy? Now he was living here on the ranch, still without a memory of who he was and where he'd come from. If Luke died, how would that affect him?

# CHAPTER TWELVE

Ben was first up, tidying the mattress and rugs away into a comfy seating area in the corner of the room. He opened up the stove and saw there was enough of a glow there to save it, ready for the morning coffee. So, Ben brought in some fuel and soon had the stove roaring into life. Ben's next chore was to get water and fill the coffeepot. Josh got up to join him and, taking the beans from the boy, began grinding them. There was the wonderful aroma of coffee now pervading the room.

"I'm always up first. I like the morning, don't you, Josh?"

Josh didn't know if he was a morning person or not, so he muttered a reply.

"Do you feel better, Josh?" The voice came from Amy, who had risen and was now walking out into the room to join them. She had slept behind the other door in the cabin.

"Yes, Amy, I feel much better. My head doesn't seem to ache so much, and I no longer feel giddy when I move." He smiled at the girl.

Amy was still sleepy and hadn't fixed her hair into its usual braids. It tumbled down her back. The long, brown hair had a gentle wave and, with her brown eyes, she looked so feminine compared to her usual appearance. Unaware of his surprise at her sleepy look, Amy, with a deft twist of her hair, had it up and positioned in a bun at the base of her neck with a couple of pins. Josh had thought Amy to be about fifteen years of age, not much older than Ben. He must have been more muddle-headed yesterday than he'd thought, because she was nearer nineteen years old, and a young woman, not the child he'd originally thought she was. Amy was not only a young woman, but she was also a very attractive one, and Josh felt an interest in her that was completely unexpected.

"Pa, shall I bring your coffee in for you?" Amy said at her father's bedroom door, knocking on it lightly. She must've heard a reply, because she opened the door and poked her head inside.

"Are you staying in bed longer, Pa? Do you want anything to eat?" There was a mumbled reply which Ben and Josh could not hear properly. Amy closed the door and walked over to them. She looked at Ben and shook her head. "Pa wants nothing to eat, just a cup of coffee. He'll rest for a while before he gets up. He doesn't look good today, Ben."

Josh didn't know what to say. Newly arrived and thrust into this family, he had noticed their difficulties in a very short time. He liked Luke, admired the man, but wondered at him and his reasons for disrupting the lives of his children for his health. From what he could gather, the doctor had given the man a death sentence. Moving to the dry desert air could only prolong it for months. But Luke had taken that chance and they were here now, a young boy and a young girl facing an uncertain future, without their father, in an area renowned to be hard and unforgiving.

"I'll take Pa's coffee into him. Ben, it's my day to go to the general store. Can you think of anything you need? Think about it whilst I speak to Pa."

Ben went over to the books and papers that were piled on the shelf, ready for his next homework. He took an envelope, already addressed, and folded and slipped inside a couple of sheets of paper. Josh could see both pages were closely written, and, to his eyes, in Ben's best handwriting. Ben looked up at Josh and put a finger to his lips. The boy didn't want Amy to know about this, thought Josh.

Breakfast was over: biscuits, refried beans, and bacon had gone down well. A knock at the door was followed by the entrance of Ezra. "Good morning, Josh. You look better this morning." At Josh's nod and smile, Ezra turned towards Amy, who asked him: "Just the usual provisions? Nothing else today?"

"Leah says she only wants her usual shop today," was Ezra's reply.

Josh spoke up. "Should I go with you, Amy? Perhaps I should go with you into the town and see if anybody knows me there."

"What if the only people that know you there are the ones that left you for dead? You don't know who they are, you could walk straight up to your killer. No, Josh, I think it's best to stay here and leave it to Amy to find out what she can about these bank robbers." Luke had come out of the bedroom and stood looking at Josh with a rueful smile. "I'm sorry. It may mean a boring stay here. But I think it's best to be careful. We must make sure those killers are far away before you venture into town."

"But what if Josh has already been in town? Someone may remember him. Perhaps he went to the general store or the saloon. There may well be somebody in town looking for him," Amy said, looking at her father in consternation. "We may find out who he is!"

There was silence for a moment, then Luke nodded his head. "Yes, maybe it's best you check it out, Josh. But take care. You could walk slap bang up to a man who thought he'd left you for dead!"

# CHAPTER THIRTEEN

Amy checked over the remaining provisions on the shelf beside the stove. "Have we..." Her voice tailed off as she turned to look at her father.

"Yes, Amy, we have enough cash left to buy goods for some time. As long as you take care and economise whilst buying." Luke rose from the table and walked into the bedroom that was his alone. He closed the door firmly behind him.

Josh watched Amy as she stood holding different packets one after the other in her hand, frowning as she decided what next to buy that would not be too expensive. Amy was far too young to live this sort of life, Josh thought. Most girls her age would think of new dresses, ribbons for their hair, and interesting outings. He moved uneasily. The injuries to his back and shoulder were improving daily; however, they stiffened up on sitting too long, and were still nagging him when he did too much physical exercise. Even his headaches were lessening, but he still had no returning memory. Those initial glimpses that he'd originally experienced had disappeared. The blank nothingness of his past was overwhelming, even frightening. The return of Luke, who handed some money over to Amy, interrupted Josh's thoughts.

"Josh could go into the saloon and the general store, but make sure that you avoid the sheriff's office," Luke said.

"Avoid the sheriff's office? Why?" Josh puzzled over that remark and gazed at Luke in astonishment as he realised what he meant. "You think I might be on a wanted poster? That's why you want me to avoid the sheriff!"

"No, I don't think you're wanted for anything. I wouldn't let you stay in my home if I thought that. I wouldn't trust Sheriff Cody if he ever found out that you were linked to the bank robbers, even if you had been their victim. Let's just say, avoid him!" Luke said.

They were ready to set off. Amy had gone back in to retrieve her gloves. Josh sat on the buggy, ready for the journey to town. "What's this town called? I don't think I've heard you mention its name," Josh asked Ben, who had rushed up to his side.

"It's Nowhere!" He laughed at Josh's face. "Yes, honestly, it's called Nowhere! The man who first came and built the first ever homestead said that he had arrived in the middle of nowhere. That's how it got its name!"

Josh laughed, "I think it's very fitting, me with no memory living in Nowhere!"

Ben looked round, checking that no one could see him. He pulled an envelope out of his pocket and thrust it into Josh's hands. "Please post this for me. Don't let Amy see it." Ben gave Josh a coin. "It was my birthday money." Josh took Ben's letter and coin and thrust them deep into the pocket of the borrowed duster coat he was wearing. An offering from Luke to keep the dust off him on the journey ahead. It was a trifle big and shabby, but he was thankful for the loan of it. Josh nodded at the boy, who looked relieved and thankful, and stepped back to help his sister climb aboard.

"We must get our story right. You are a cousin of ours? Is that what Pa said?" Amy asked Josh as they rode across the deserted landscape.

"Yes, I think I should be a distant cousin. Otherwise, Ben would have mentioned me before now. I know!

There was an argument, and it estranged my family from your side of the family. Would that make sense?" Josh suggested.

"I don't know if that makes sense or not. Let's not get too complicated, we will only get muddled up. Yes, I think that would work. You are from a distant branch of the family that has been estranged from our branch for many years. You wanted to come and look at the Wild West, because you thought of settling down here, and so looked up my father. Will that do?" Amy said and looked at the expression on Josh's face.

"Yes, that's great. But what about my past? What about where I've been? And what I have been doing? Do you think I'll be asked those sorts of questions?"

"No! No one asks those sorts of questions. It's not done out West, and if you asked them, you might get a bullet in reply!" Amy said.

They drove on for some time in silence. But it was a companionable silence. Josh realised he felt at ease with this family. Somehow, he knew it differed from the family relationships he had had in the past. How he knew that, he didn't know. He was involved with this family, whether he wanted it or not. But this increasing involvement was not something he wished to shy away from. Josh wanted to help, and he especially wanted to lessen the load on Amy's shoulders. His growing feelings for the girl were worrying. Surely a man with no name, no past, and possibly no future, should not get too close to Amy?

"There it is! The town of Nowhere. We have the saloon, a general store, a livery stable, and the hotel. They are not what you would expect in a normal town. They built the general store with logs. The livery stable is an old dwelling made of adobe. But they made the saloon up of tents, and they are still trying to build a permanent building. The so-called hotel is also made up of tents, it's being added to all the time. It's amazing how fast some of these properties have risen. Sometimes it's only days before a business takes off. Then it goes again, as the owner moves on to somewhere busier."

Amy drove up to the general store. She jumped down and hitched the reins to the post before turning to Josh. "Do you want to go into the saloon whilst I get the provisions? I'll have them ready for you to help me out with them to the buggy."

Josh jumped down, then stood looking at her. He felt himself go red with embarrassment. How the hell could he ask this young girl for money? It was only when he had looked across at the saloon that he realised he did not have a single coin to his name.

Amy had reached for the bag under the seat where she'd been sitting and pulled out her cloth purse. The coins within it were jingling. "Oh! You have no money. How stupid of me, and how embarrassing for you. Here, I don't know how much you have to pay in the saloon. Take this, and remember: don't tell people too much, but listen to whatever gossip you can hear."

Josh took the coins and slipped them into his pocket. He, too, was unaware of what a drink cost, but he would make certain that it would be the cheapest he could buy. No way would he squander their money. He walked up the steps, across the porch, and pushed open the swing doors. The front of the saloon looked like every other saloon, but it was a false front giving an air of permanence to the building. Behind that false front was a tent. A long table at the back of the tent held the usual bar stuff. Before it, some stools were drawn up to the table. Also dotted around the room were round, rough-hewn tables with stools. A few men sat at one table. Their talk ceased as Josh walked in. Conscious of all eyes on him, Josh walked straight up to the bar and looked at the man behind it.

"What have you got? And how much?" he asked the man who stood looking Josh up and down. Josh noted the gun slung casually but prominently on his hip, the large, meaty fists, and the broken nose of the older man. Age may have crept up on him, but Josh knew that this was a man you didn't argue with. He looked mean and capable of holding his own in any bar fight. And, Josh thought, he probably came out the winner.

Josh took the cheapest drink and sat down to drink it on the nearest stool. It was warm, and had a watery taste, but it was wet and he was dry from the journey from the ranch. Josh drank some of it and wiped his mouth with his hand. He was conscious of the eyes of the other men in the bar upon him.

"Ain't seen you around here before. Passing through?" the bartender asked him. He had a dirty cloth in his hand with which he was polishing a glass. His eyes were fixed upon Josh with a suspicious, intent stare. The atmosphere in this bar made Josh uneasy. He gulped more of the drink, eager to get it finished and out of the bar.

Josh was aware of the conversation ceasing behind him. The men at the table had stopped to listen to what he had to say. "Yes, first time visiting my folks. Uncle moved into Broken Horseshoe Ranch a while ago."

"That's the guy who moved out here because he's sick," the bartender replied, hoping to prompt Josh into further revelations. "You give him a hand or what?"

"Yes," Josh replied. He drained the glass, placing it back down on the table. Standing up, he gave the bartender a nod. "Thanks," and walked out of the tent onto the dusty main street of Nowhere. He didn't recognise anyone in the saloon, and no one recognised him. As Josh stood there, the realisation that he may never know who he really was, or where he came from, hit him hard. For a while, he stared at the township of Nowhere and felt nothing. An emptiness crept inside his soul, and he didn't know what to do next. What was he? Who was he?

# CHAPTER FOURTEEN

"Josh! Josh, over here!" Amy's voice cut through the miasma of thought that was going round and round in his head. She waved at him before placing a parcel in the buggy. "Come on over and help me." Amy went back into the store.

Josh stood looking up and down the dusty, flat piece of ground that was Main Street in Nowhere. A woman carried a small bag as she came out of the general store. She looked at him and hurriedly looked away before trotting down the street towards one of the few buildings and entering one of them. There were voices in the livery stable and the sound of a blacksmith working. Probably on a horseshoe, thought Josh. A sudden swirl of the scorching desert wind caused dust to eddy about him. No, he didn't recognise this place. No one in the saloon knew him, so he crossed over to join Amy at the store.

He nodded at the man and woman serving at the store before helping Amy with the heavier provisions. On his return to fetch the last of the heavy sacks that Amy had bought, the owner of the store came across to him. "Hello, Amy says you're a cousin. Come out here to help and get to know how we live out here in the West. I'm Manuel. I own this store." They shook hands, Josh realising that the swarthy barrel-chested man with a slight Mexican accent was a stranger to him. The man hitched up his baggy canvas trousers, his braces struggling to keep them over the enormous belly. He called to his wife. "Hey, Eliza, come and meet this young man. By your accent, you've come from the East." The man guffawed at this, finding it a huge joke.

The little woman that joined them gave Josh a

cheerful smile from a round moon face with button black eyes, and hair wound round in a plait on top of her head. "That family could do with a hand helping them out. I know Amy and Ben put in more than their fair share on that ranch. Good to see you, young man. Hope you enjoy your stay here. Never know, you might make Nowhere your home." Eliza shook hands with him and gave him another beaming smile before turning away to sort out the shelves behind her. Whilst Amy was out at the buggy, Josh handed Manuel the letter that Ben had given to him to post. Josh breathed a sigh of relief when he actually got change back from the coin Ben had handed to him. As Manuel placed it into a canvas sack ready to be sorted for whichever method by which the post left Nowhere, Josh wished the letter well.

"Nothing," Josh said, as he came out of the store and climbed onto the buggy with Amy for the return home. "No one knows me and I don't recognise them or this place."

Amy turned to him to speak, but whirled around as there were shouts and cries outside the hotel. Again, it was a makeshift building, quickly flung up with a lopsided sign burned into a large piece of wood. **"Beds. Food**." Its message was plain and simple! From what Josh remembered Ezra telling him, it was just basically beds and a large cookhouse.

A man was shaking something as he pulled it out of the door. "Useless! Waste of money I spent on your fare. Starve on the street for all I care. No use to me with a broken arm!"

A few people on the street halted, and some walked curiously towards the source of the noise. It was a small Chinese boy who had been flung onto the ground. The man standing over him was a mean-looking weasel of a man. He shook his fist threatening at the boy. "Don't come to my place again. Useless..."

Before Josh realised what was happening, Amy had rushed over and was standing between the boy and the man. "Leave him alone. He's hurt!"

"I can do with him what I want. He's mine! I paid for his fare out here. I expected a man from the advert to work in my kitchen. What do I get? A useless boy. He can't carry the heavy pots and is no good at cooking over a fire. Now he's got a broken arm." The man shouted all this at Amy and the boy and then raised a fist threateningly towards the girl.

"Don't you touch her!" Josh was beside Amy, who was helping the small boy to his feet. Josh's voice was soft, but he looked at the man with such ferocious intent in his voice and with such an expression on his face that the man drew back and his fist went down to his side.

"He's mine. I paid his fare out here." The man still glowered at the boy who shrank away from him beside Amy, sensing an unexpected protector in her.

"What was his fare? I'll pay it and he can be mine," Amy said, and began rummaging in her purse.

Josh saw the crafty look cross the man's face. "The right fare, not a penny more," Josh said, again in the quiet, forceful tone. Before the man could reply, a voice shouted from behind Josh, telling him the actual fare. Amy looked at Josh, gave him a thankful nod, fished out the correct money and handed it to the man. She called a "thank you" to the man who had called out the right price.

Amy looked at the weasel man but said nothing. She had been out West for only a short time, but she knew when it was best to walk away. She grabbed the boy's good wrist and walked with him towards the buggy. Josh looked at the man and the few spectators that were now drifting away and followed Amy, a grin on his face. What would Luke say when she arrived back at the ranch with yet another stray person she had found? Three! That was a saying he remembered. Everything goes in threes! He was looking forward to the third waif and stray that Amy would find and take back to the ranch with her.

"Let's get you up in the buggy. What's your name?" Amy had moved the provisions to one side in the buggy and pulled some sacking into a cushioned spot for the boy.

Josh watched her for a moment and then reached forward to help the boy up into the buggy. He was horrified to see the extent of the burns and cuts upon the boy. A tattered shirt barely covered the emaciated body, and a broken arm hung at his side. The black hair was cut in a jagged manner across the back of his head. No doubt he had worn a pigtail which had been hacked off. No wonder Amy felt sorry for the boy. Bending down, Josh lifted the boy into the buggy, taking care not to jar the wounded arm. He looked closely at the arm. When they reached the ranch, he'd have time to sort it out. Not here, not while the man was watching. Josh was certain that the arm was not broken, only dislocated.

The boy lifted his head and his eyes held fear and apprehension of what was about to happen to him now. Amy must have realised, because she bent forward and patted the young boy on his good arm. "Don't worry, we won't hurt you. You're coming to my home. I have a brother about your age. We have a ranch, and you can help him about the place. That's all you have to do. When we get back, I'll sort out those wounds. I'm Amy, and this is Josh."

"Chan, I am Chan," the whisper reached their ears. Josh thought the boy understood most of what Amy had told him because the look of fear had been replaced by one of hope.

They both climbed upon the buggy and Josh smiled at Amy. "What will your father say to your arrival with yet another injured soul?"

"He'll say that it was the right thing to do. It was a Christian thing to do." Amy's reply came with a hesitancy showing that she was uncertain of how her father would take to Chan's arrival.

"I'm looking forward to the third one," Josh said.

"The third one?" Amy questioned him as she manoeuvred along the road leading out of Nowhere.

"Everything comes in threes! First you found me, now you buy Chan. I can't wait to see what or who number three is!"

# CHAPTER FIFTEEN

"Amy's coming! She's got someone with her. They are not alone!" The distance was difficult to judge, Josh thought. The shimmering heat, the dust kicked up by the horse and the wheels of the buggy, and the brilliant sun shining into his face made him squint. But they heard Ben's shouts from some distance away. As they drew nearer to the ranch, Ben ran out to meet them. "Who's this, Amy? Why have you brought him here?"

The buggy drew to a stop, the final swirl of the dust around it making them all cough. It was Amy who jumped down first to rush over to her father and explain the situation. "I found him on the street. That Joe who runs the cookhouse had thrown him out. He's broken his arm and is no use in the kitchen. The boy is covered in burns from cooking. Joe said he got him from an advert in a newspaper just for the payment of his fare. Said he'd sell him to anyone who'd got the fare money. Folks were walking round him and ignoring him. I couldn't let the boy starve. So I gave Joe the fare for the boy. I don't know what to do about his arm, though." Leah and Ben joined Luke and Amy and crowded round the buggy, and watched as Ezra and Josh helped the young boy down from the wagon. In obvious pain, the Chinese boy stood shaking visibly as they crowded around him.

"Oh, you poor boy! Come and sit on the step here." Amy took his good arm and guided him towards the porch steps, gesturing him to sit. There was an appalled silence as each of them took in the shaking little boy, covered with burns and welts, his one arm hanging uselessly at his side. He looked at them, confusion in his eyes. But as they all watched, his small hand – the good one – reached out to clasp Amy's hand.

"He's Chinese, isn't he? Can he speak English? He looks nearly the same age as me," said Ben, walking forward, looking down at the boy and smiling at him.

"Hasn't said a word since we told him to sit up in the wagon. The jolts over the rough ground made him gasp a few times. I think he's in terrible pain with that arm. What can we do about it?" Amy pressed the hand in hers comfortingly even as she shook her head in despair.

"Here, have a drink of water." Ben produced a cup of water, which he gave to the boy. He took it in his good hand, all the while gazing up at them. He drank some and handed it back with a nod of thanks.

"No one else knows what to do with that arm?" Josh asked them. Every head shook in denial. "Still haven't got my memory back. But I know what to do here, though. Strange business, this memory thing. Ben, go behind the lad and hold his good shoulder. Luke, you got any whiskey or brandy? He's going to need it!" Josh looked down at the boy. "I'm going to hurt you. It will be bad! Immediately after, the pain will gradually clear away and your arm will be as good as new." Josh saw a fleeting look of comprehension on the boy's face. He knows English, even if he can't speak it. Shall I tell the others? No, I'll let the lad have his secret. For now.

The boy stood in front of Josh, with an apprehensive Ben standing behind him. Luke had come out with a small tot of whiskey in a tin cup. Josh took a deep breath, trying to remember all that he had seen when this operation had been carried out in front of him. He couldn't remember where or who to, but he remembered how to do it. It was over. He had twisted the arm, pulling it out straight until the joint slid into place. Chan had screamed and fainted into Ben's arms. Josh picked the lightweight up and carried him into the cabin, placing him on the mattress in the corner. Luke followed and watched the boy as he gradually seemed to wake up for a moment, glanced round at them, and then fell asleep. Luke shrugged and emptied the tin cup.

"I couldn't leave the boy. Chinese aren't welcome in this town. Only someone like Joe, who would work them every hour God sends, welcomes them. I brought him here, didn't know what else to do with him." Amy's voice tailed off, and she looked round at the others, especially her father.

"Nothing else you could do, Amy. You did a good thing. Couldn't leave him there. He'd probably have starved to death," Ezra said.

"Yes, Amy, it was the Christian thing to do. But now we have another mouth to feed!" Luke said wearily as he walked into the bedroom, closing the door behind him.

"Any news in town, Amy?" Ezra asked as they unloaded the goods from the wagon onto the table. Amy took the packets and tins and carefully placed them in their allotted places on her shelves. "Did you hear anything?"

"It was bad news. Those men were real killers. How you survived, Josh, I don't know. They tried to rob a coach. Somehow, they knew it was carrying gold to pay soldiers. There was a real shootout, but they came off worst. After they rode away, it was discovered they had killed the family living nearby at the livery stables where the coaches stop to change horses. Everyone in that family, including the children, was killed. The guards on the coach shot and killed two of the bandits, and they wounded another couple of them. They got away with some of the gold, and it's reckoned they're heading into the hills and perhaps down to Mexico when they've shaken off their pursuers."

"How did I come to be mixed up with them?" Josh said, staring at the flames in the stove without seeing them. "Was I one of them? Could I have been a killer? I don't feel like one." Josh thought that was a stupid remark to make and sat down on a chair with a thump.

"Don't think you're a killer, Josh. You don't act like one," Ezra said.

"How do killers act?" was Josh's reply. "How would I know if I was a killer?"

# CHAPTER SIXTEEN

During the day, Ben had taken the Chinese boy around the ranch, showing him everything. Ben talked, pointing and explaining, and Chan nodded and smiled. He had woken up from his rest, astonished – as everyone else had been – to find his arm working and back to normal but for the terrible, achy pain within it.

Josh smiled when the boy walked up to him, gave a bow, and said, "thank you." Then Chan turned and walked up to Amy and repeated the same actions. The morning had passed with the usual chores being undertaken. Ben spent most of his time with the horses. They had three horses in total. One was an elderly chestnut belonging to Ezra. The other two had been purchased by Luke on his arrival at the ranch. Bella was Amy's favourite. They were adequate for their tasks of routine visits to town and Amy's excursions. They could have been thoroughbreds, though, for the care and attention that Ben lavished on them.

Luke stood over his pathetic attempt at a vegetable patch in the afternoon. "I help?" Chan had come up behind Luke and, for a moment, had watched him.

"Yes, Chan, if you can help I would be glad of it," was the weary reply.

"Water!" Chan said and, taking the spade from the willing hands of Luke, the boy started digging a channel towards the spring. A few more channels branching out from the initial one were dug in quick succession. "Water for many plants. They thirsty!"

Luke had sent off for some seeds and they had arrived the previous week. He had been looking at them earlier and they were spread out on the bench on the porch. Chan had watched Luke look at them, and when Luke had turned away to go to the garden, the boy had checked over them himself.

"I plant seeds?" Chan asked Luke. The boy waved the seeds enthusiastically and smiled up at the man.

"Yes, I don't know what I'm doing, so I'll be very pleased if you take charge of them," the older man said, looking down at the enthusiastic face of the young boy.

Chan placed the seeds out in small rows, then showed that Ben should push them into the soil. Each packet was noted and only a small amount of seed planted. "Later, we plant some for later." Chan folded over the seed packets carefully and ran back to the porch, where he placed them neatly for Luke. The two boys continued whilst Luke watched with a smile on his face. Soon, there was an area of freshly turned soil, planted with neat rows of seeds, and the two boys were watering them with a tin full of water, its bottom peppered with holes.

Josh watched, the smell of the newly turned earth rose into his nostrils. It had a sandy, earthy smell, one that was new to him. Then, when the water landed on the parched earth, it almost sizzled as the heat caused it to evaporate. Josh inhaled the new earth smell and wondered at how such small things could mean so much to him. Did the man he had been before take time and show interest in such little things?

That evening, Josh watched the others as they relaxed after the day's toil. Ben's enthusiastic speech as he explained the intricacies of his books to Chan could be heard as the others sat quietly drinking their coffee, thinking about the last few days' hectic events.

Then Amy brought the topic up. "I want to go out again tomorrow. What do you say, Pa?" she sent her father a quizzical look and then looked towards Josh.

"What do you think, Ezra? Do we trust this man?" Luke asked the old-timer. Luke took Ezra's advice seriously and always acted upon it, Josh realised. He wondered what the old man would say. Did Ezra trust him? Did Josh trust himself? That was a problem that was keeping him awake at night.

"Yes, I think we can. You've told him the story, and he can go with Amy tomorrow. That way, she'll have company with her. I'll get that young lad sorted out. He's showing an interest and seems to take everything we say into his head. Maybe I can get him working for us and helping us out. That way, he will pay his way."

"Yes, Ezra, I think you're right. That's what we'll do tomorrow. Take care, Amy. Josh, you watch out for her." Luke gave them a smile, which was another weak one, and then went off to bed.

"He's getting weaker, isn't he, Ezra?" Amy's whisper fell into the awkward silence that had followed Luke's departure.

The old man looked at the girl, and Josh could see the tears in his eyes, but he rallied valiantly to smile at the girl. "It's only natural. Some days he has good days, others are not so good. Maybe he'll feel fitter tomorrow." Rising to his feet, Ezra patted her on the shoulder and went out of the door. Before the door closed behind him, he popped his head back in. "Reckon that young lad could stay in our place. Though I reckon young Ben's taken a shine to him and wants him in here with you lot. Josh, I think we'd better build on another room for this ranch. Shouldn't take us long now we've got you here." Ezra gave them his gummy grin and went off to bed.

"I'll go to bed now. It's an early start in the morning.

Will you be fit enough, Josh?" Amy got up from the bench and walked towards her bedroom door.

Josh assured her he would be fine in the morning and told her to go to bed. "I'll settle the two young ones down for the night." He had seen the tears in her eyes and knew that she needed time alone to process the obvious decline of her father.

"Thank you, Josh. I'll go in and read the walls." Amy opened the door of her tiny cupboard room.

"You read the walls?" Josh asked, puzzled at that last remark.

"Yes, come and have a look." Amy opened the door wider, and Josh peered in over her shoulder. It was just a large cupboard. Her mattress lay on one side of the wall, a couple of small shelves were beside it. She had books and a small mirror and brush. Her few clothes hung on pegs. But what caught his attention were the walls themselves. They had decorated the adobe walls, papering them and sticking newspapers on them for both warmth and decoration.

"But the news must be getting stale by now!" He joked. He felt delighted when she laughed at him. Somehow, it seemed such a silly remark, but her entire face lit up and for a moment she looked the young and carefree girl that she should have been every moment of her day.

It was early. Amy had told him she left the ranch before dawn, whilst it was still cool. Josh awoke feeling so much better, but wasn't sure about the early morning ride. The two boys had shared a mattress last night, and whilst there had been a few giggles and scuffles from Ben at first, they had both slept deeply. Josh had a quick look at Chan's arm. It seemed so much better, and he had more movement back in it. The pain had obviously diminished and the burns that they had attended to yesterday no longer looked so angry or raw. The boy's face had a new look, not quite hope, but the fearful, downtrodden look he had worn yesterday seemed to have lessened.

"Do we have a cup of coffee before we go?" Josh asked Amy. He wasn't sure he could go without his coffee.

"Yes, I always need a coffee before setting out."

Ben rose from his mattress, wearily rubbed his eyes, and staggered out of the cabin. "He's getting the horses ready for us. I'll pack some of yesterday's biscuits and slice some of yesterday's cold bacon to eat on the way. Fill this canteen up with water, and I'll do mine. Make sure you have a good drink before we leave of water and coffee!"

They rode off into the cool morning air, the rising sun at their backs. At a certain point where the land rose, Amy paused and turned to look back at the ranch. She took off her hat and waved it. Josh followed her gaze to see Ben and Ezra waving their hats in return and, behind them, a tiny figure. The Chinese boy was also waving both hands in the air. Josh smiled at the sight as they rode off towards the Devil's Mountain to search for Jesuit gold.

# CHAPTER SEVENTEEN

Josh felt that the overpowering heat was even thrown up from the surrounding ground. With every step they took, they could feel the heat rising even through their boots. Inhaling, the very air seemed to burn into their lungs. "There's shade behind that rock. We'll sit awhile and have a drink," Amy said, steering a course towards the shade. They had been walking the horses while they looked for a spot to rest. The rock hung over a depression in the rocky ground. Walking their horses into the shade in the deepest part of the depression, they both sank down with their backs against the rock.

"There's been nothing to find so far. I think this area is now a waste of time," Amy said with a dejected sigh.

"From looking at the map that Luke had this morning, I think heading towards the hills in a straight line from the cactus markings might be worth looking at," Josh said, taking the hat from his head and wiping the sweat that dripped down from his blonde hair. He noticed that his hand shook, and the water revived him only a little. He nibbled on the hard biscuits that Amy had brought with them. They had eaten the cold bacon slices earlier that morning. Why did he feel so weak he wondered? One thing he remembered was that he had been fitter than he now felt.

"Rest another few minutes, and then we'll head for home. It's too late to start a new search and you're still suffering from your injuries," Amy said.

Josh wanted to argue with her. He'd felt that his idea of their next search was a good one. He'd like to get started right away. But the energy of the morning was gone. It was time to be sensible. Amy could clearly see the weakness that was still lingering within him.

"I'd like to say that you are mistaken and I'm keen to start another search, but you're right, Amy. I feel tired, and it makes me mad having to say so!" Josh said through gritted teeth.

Amy's peals of laughter echoed round the shady spot they were in. Astounded, Josh could only stare at her. "You sound like my Pa, and my brother. They both hate feeling tired or sick. Let's go home now. If you're keen to look over that way, how about we leave even earlier tomorrow morning and get a good start on the day before it gets too hot?" Amy suggested.

Hating to leave the cool shade of the rock, they set off back to the ranch. The last time he had been on this route back to the Broken Horseshoe Ranch, he had been nearly unconscious and had staggered most of the way. Now, on horseback and feeling, if not completely recovered, certainly much better than he had been, he took stock of the countryside about him. Behind him and to the left were the Devil's Mountain and other smaller peaks. Harsh peaks of rock rose jaggedly into the sky. It was a cruel, forbidding landscape and, in the heat of the day, the temperature soared, making it almost unbearable to move. The wildlife of the region took shelter, hiding in the shady spots they could find, underground, beneath rocks, and in the many crevices and caves. They had been at the very edge of the mountains and now they were descending into the flat desert plain.

The Broken Horseshoe Ranch lay at the very foothills of the Devil's Mountain. As they descended, they reached the last rocky outcrop of the hills and could look down on the desert stretching before them. Broken Horseshoe Ranch and its ramshackle outbuildings lay with their backs to a small canyon. A spring at the edge of the canyon supplied it with fresh water. A few miles away, Josh could see another ranch. Somehow, even with the distance, it looked neater and more prosperous than Amy's home.

"There's two buggies outside the ranch! That large one belongs to Widow Perkins." Amy sat up high in the saddle, shading her eyes from the sun. "I think the other one belongs to the Preacher." There was an instant alarm in her voice, and Amy was overwhelmed with fear. Josh could see it in her face. "It must be Pa! Something must have happened to him!" Amy was about to set off in her blind panic and race towards the ranch.

Josh leant forward and put his hand on hers. "No, Amy! Not like this!" Josh's voice was firm but kindly. "It's no good racing the horse wildly through this terrain. Either the horse will come to grief or you will. We return to the ranch calmly. There is no need to injure the horse or yourself. That will do your father no good at all."

The sensible words Josh uttered left his mouth with mixed feelings. He didn't know Amy well enough to judge her reaction. Would she race off, heedless of what he had said? Or would she heed his warning? He suddenly realised his hand was still on hers, but pressed it gently in a reassuring manner.

Amy didn't draw her hand away from his touch. Instead, she looked down at it, and then returned the pressure for a moment and gave him a weak smile. "Thank you, Josh. You make sense. I might not appreciate it and would love to race home, but I lamed one horse the other day. Poor old Bella does not deserve the same treatment!"

The smile she gave Josh was genuine, but it was a

worried smile, and she urged her horse forward, and took up a steady pace homewards. The anxious frown on her face grew ever deeper the nearer they got to the ranch.

"Yes, that's Widow Perkins and the Preacher. What can they want? I don't think it can be anything good. I know Pa's been ill, but I hoped he was improving. The doctor said he would improve if we could get him into the hot, dry air of the desert lands. What can they want? Why are they here? What's happened?"

# CHAPTER EIGHTEEN

Never would Josh forget that ride. Eager to spur the horses into further fast action, they both somehow kept a steady pace. The ranch shimmered in the distant heat of the sun like a mirage. It was there, but never seemed to get any nearer. Amy edged ahead of Josh and he let his gaze fix upon her back, the tension in her shoulders evident to his gaze. He knew she was anxious about what awaited them. He, too, was worried. Life was precarious in this part of the world for anyone, let alone a girl and her young brother. He had no memory, so how could he help if the worst had happened?

The figures on the porch waved at them, and both the riders could see her father standing tall and straight. No sign of a collapse there, thought Josh. He noted the figure beside him. A large roly-poly of a woman, with a huge, white-haired bun on top of her head. White hair was escaping wildly from its confines, and with the sun behind her, gave her the appearance of a halo.

"He looks all right! Pa isn't ill." Amy uttered these words with a gasping squeak, forced out of her in a rush of relief.

"Who's the large woman?" Josh had to ask, certain that he should get all the information about the woman before he arrived.

"Widow Perkins, she's the one the sheriff was going to call in on yesterday. Her land is next to ours. She's lived there for some time. Her husband died a couple of years back from a snake bite and she works at it herself with a Mexican family. She never goes calling anywhere. I wonder what she wants."

Neither spoke, they just rode on, the figures becoming

clearer now. The other person who Josh could see was a tall, well-built man. He didn't look happy at all. Even from a distance, Josh could see a mournful expression on the man's face.

Ben rushed towards them, taking the horses and leading them to the lean to stable. The horses were his province. He always looked after them and cared for them. Ben stretched towards his sister as he took her horse and whispered in her ear. "Widow Perkins wouldn't say why she was here until you arrived home. What can it be about? Why has she ridden over here with that preacher man?"

Both Josh and Amy stood for a moment, brushing the dust from their clothes before mounting the steps up to the porch. To their surprise, the little Chinese boy rushed out towards them, carefully carrying two brimming cups of coffee. He handed them over, then backed away and rushed back into the cabin.

"Little chap is keen to please us. Seems like he wants to stay here, and this is his way of making himself useful," Luke said and smiled after the departing boy.

"I hear you are Luke's nephew. Welcome, Josh, to this desolate hole." Widow Perkins stuck out her calloused, hard-skinned hand and shook the hand Josh proffered. He winced. The unexpectedly tough grasp had surprised him. "Now then, everyone is here. I'll speak about why I've come visiting like this."

Josh was hoping the porch was strong enough to support the crowd of people that were sitting on it. Ben had been joined by Chan and both sat on the lower steps. Ezra and Leah sat on the top step. They both looked worried and uncomfortable. The Preacher sat gingerly on a three-legged stool, whilst Amy joined her father on the bench. Josh stood, his back against the wall, surveying with great interest the assembled crowd.

The large woman that was the Widow Perkins stood and faced them all. Her hands went on her hips, and she gazed around thoughtfully, eyeing each one of them, checking to see that they were listening properly. With amusement, Josh thought, never had anybody such a rapt audience. Not one of them was fidgeting or interested in anything other than what the Widow Perkins was about to say.

"As you all know, Sheriff Cody called in on me yesterday. To warn me about some bank robbers was his excuse. I dislike the man and I don't trust him. When he gets off his horse, he doesn't look at me. He surveys my property with the eye of a man who wishes to own it. I fear he is going to make me an offer of marriage." She waved away the gasps and exclamations of her audience. "I know he has that floozy in town, whom no doubt he would install after he has married, and perhaps buried, me!" This time, when she expected a reaction, there was none. Her audience had been stunned into silence by this last remark. Even the Widow Perkins seemed shy of making her next remarks to them, because she halted. She moved a little uneasily, one foot on the other. Her hands began to twist and turn, and she gratefully grabbed the belt around her waist and fiddled with it.

"I don't want to marry him, and I don't want to see him at my ranch. So I have a proposition to make. I want everything open and above board with all of you, that's why I wanted you all here present. I propose that Luke and I get wed." She raised her hand to stop the outcry of gasps and interruptions. "A marriage of convenience. The Preacher is here to do it. We have enough witnesses present to make it legal. Then I wish to draw up a will in front of all of you, leaving my land and the ranch to Ben and Amy. This way, that rascally sheriff can't get his hands on my property!"

# CHAPTER NINETEEN

The silence seemed to go on forever before the Preacher got to his feet. It was a hard movement as his long legs seemed to fight with the three legs of the stool as he tried to gain his balance.

"I will not perform any marriage ceremony if either party is unwilling. I have to be assured that both are entering this holy state of matrimony and are willing and keen to become marriage partners."

"Amy, what do you think of my idea?" The large, rotund woman shot the question unexpectedly at Amy, who reared back, startled. "It will affect you most, my dear. I can help you out with my animals and my workers. You will find life easier, and you will have the security of knowing that if the worst happens to your father – forgive me, Luke, if I speak plain – you will have the security of myself and the Dry Creek Ranch behind you."

"Well, Amy, it seems my prospective bride has given you the deciding vote as to whether I should get wed again or not," was Luke's dry remark to his daughter.

"What do you think, Pa? You will be the one getting wed," retorted Amy.

The Widow Perkins continued speaking. "I think everything would go on as before. I continue living at my place and you all continue living here. The only differences will be legal and financial. I shall not be pursued by that slob of a sheriff, and your children will have the added security of my backing and that of my ranch." She stood, her arms folded across her ample bosom, and waited for their answers.

"Yes," said Luke.

"This is all you have to say, Pa? Just 'yes'?" Amy asked her father, astonished at his brief reply.

"That's all I need to say!" her father replied with a slight smile. "The widow talks sense. I have often worried how you and Ben will manage without me. I'd no longer have that worry and she would have no more problems with the sheriff. It's a good deal! Especially for you and Ben, you would both have a future secured for you."

"Then I suggest you get us wed, Preacher!" said the prospective bride. Then she added, "you'd better all start calling me 'Nancy'."

Josh became the best man, and Amy gave the bride away. Nancy, hoping that her request would be accepted, had come prepared with food for a wedding feast. Broken Horseshoe Ranch that evening was the unexpected centre of bridal festivities. Mexican food from Nancy's ranch appeared with Leah's help. A delicious spread was set out on the table. Plates and platters were filled, and each carried them out to sit on the porch, or some workers sat on the ground enjoying the unexpected feast. Boiled ham, pickles and relishes, and Mexican fare were joined with pies, cornbread, and Leah's chilli. Because the Preacher was staying for the meal and the signing of the will which he'd written out in front of them, no alcohol was served. Water and coffee washed the food down.

Nancy took Amy to one side and put her arm round the girl's shoulder. "You've had a hard time of it since you moved out here. I've watched you. You've taken it all in your stride and made the best of everything. Now, you've got me. I'll be ready to help you whenever you need it. Don't hesitate to call on me. You and your Pa have saved me from constantly having to avoid that sheriff and his remarks. Don't want to cross the man, there's a nasty streak in him. This way, I don't have to refuse any proposal."

"Thank you, Nancy. I'm really grateful to you. We've had Leah and Ezra help us, but they are getting older and having someone like yourself near at hand, especially if..." Amy couldn't continue as the tears filled her eyes at the thought of what might happen if her father died.

"Yes, Amy, if the worst happens, I'll be here. But I'm going to make sure it doesn't happen. I don't want to be a widow any time soon! Tomorrow, I'm sending you a cow. You can milk her daily for your father, and we've got some vegetables that I'll send regularly for him. My lot are good at hunting rabbits and whatever game they can find, I reckon that can find its way over here. You'll see, good food and fresh air might well help your father to make a full recovery!"

Josh, still sitting on the step, overheard this conversation. The relief he felt surprised him. How did he get so involved with this family and their problems? To be so integrated with them in such a short time was almost frightening. Was it the whole family he worried about? Or could he be finally honest with himself and admit that it was Amy who occupied his thoughts?

# CHAPTER TWENTY

Amy was delighted to find that the earlier start they had planned for the morning had proved so successful. They were so much further on than she remembered ever being before. The map they had looked at last night with the strange symbols the Mexican had written out had been memorised. That important sentinel cactus with the ancient markings on it they had passed earlier.

"Over there, behind those small boulders, that's where I found the carved stone." Amy pointed the place out to Josh.

"You then went on to the left of that cactus. Let's ride on behind it. Further into the mountains, which would surely make more sense if you were seeking a crevice or cave to hide your gold?"

"Yes, that's true, Josh. Onward into the mountains would make more sense for them to seek hiding places. We'll rest at noon or wherever we can find some shade," said Amy.

Josh followed the girl into the higher ground. Not yet steep. The ground was rising and the gentle hills were now giving way to jagged rocks. The peaks were towering over them, the dominant feature of the Devil's Mountain.

Josh's arm was still painful and his back felt increasingly susceptible to the sudden movements of his horse. This full day's ride would not be easy on him or his injuries! He'd stick it out though, and no way would he miss out on an expedition for hidden gold. Treasure seeking had been one of the exciting games of his boyhood. Surely every boy wanted to seek treasure on islands or in caves? Josh knew instinctively that he had been such a boy.

The journey in the increasing heat was endless, and it was with difficulty that they both kept alert and conscious of their surroundings.

"Amy! Look over there." A sudden movement in the brush at the foot of the cliff had alerted Josh to danger. Had it been a lizard? Or perhaps a snake? His immediate glance to that side of the canyon had shown him a carving on a rock. "I think there's a drawing on that rock. Isn't that the symbol we were looking for? I'm going over to have a look." Josh turned his horse's head and rode nearer to the rocky cliffs at the side of the canyon. Shelves of rock were layered on top of one another and towered above the two riders as they went ever deeper into the canyons of the Devil's Mountain. This far beneath the cliff walls, the sun was cut off from their view as they progressed further into the deepening canyon.

"Josh, it's the drawings from the Mexican's map! I'm amazed you saw them from the trail. They are so well hidden here," exclaimed Amy.

"I would never have seen them if something hadn't caught my eye with its movement along the ground. We'd better take care in case it was a snake."

They tethered their horses to a patch of straggly brush that was growing up despite the lack of sunshine and water. Both walked across to stand beneath the carvings. There were several carvings, and they walked slowly, gazing up at each one individually. Only three of them were like those of the Mexican's map. "All these drawings and signs carved along the rocks go further around into this tiny cavelike opening. Do you think they were all done at the same time, Josh?"

"No, I'm certain they weren't. Look at these signs that the Mexican has carved. They look much fresher than the others. They're not weathered. I think these others are very ancient."

For some time, they walked along, staring up at the rocks, wondering what stories they were trying to tell them. "All these people carved their mark ages past. They were determined to prove that they were here. Who were they? Where were they going to? Where had they come from?" Amy said quietly, her finger gently tracing the symbol that was closest to her.

Josh watched her and smiled to himself. It was almost as if Amy was trying to get in touch with the person who carved that symbol hundreds of years ago. He continued to follow the rock wall where it curved round into a small, sheltered space. Not only was it out of the sun, but it was out of the wind, which was blowing strongly that day.

"Amy, come round here. We should take a rest here. There's plenty of shade for the horses as well as us. We can all stay out of the sun." When he returned to Amy, it was to find that she had untied both horses and was leading them towards him.

"I would have ridden past those signs. That was a good job you spotted them, Josh." Amy smiled at him as she passed him the reins of his horse.

That's what I like about this girl, Josh thought. She gave credit where it was due and didn't have to always be in the right. But I'd better give the credit to the real culprit. "Remember, I told you, it was only because I saw movement over here. Otherwise, I would have ridden past it as well."

"It could have been a rabbit. They sometimes come

out in the daytime into the shade. Could be a lizard or a snake. There are plenty of critters around here. Not all of them hide up during the day," Amy said.

Josh took a sip of water as he leant back against the rock. Amy took a small sip as well, then rummaged in her bag, bringing out some biscuits left over from Leah's baking yesterday. Hard as they may have been, they tasted good in the heat and dust as they rested in the shade.

A sudden burst of gunfire accompanied by shouts and a woman's screams rebounded from the cliff faces about them. They jumped to their feet and stared at one another. Josh took a step towards his horse as if about to dash off and investigate. Amy grabbed his arm. "Wait, we're no help to anyone! A girl and an injured man are no match for bandits!"

## CHAPTER TWENTY-ONE

The screams were cut short, and the gunfire ceased. Josh stood with his hands still on his horse's bridle. Shouts were all that could be heard now, and then horses galloping nearer to them.

"Hold the horses! Keep them quiet. They're riding up this canyon. We can't let them see us." Amy's urgent whisper galvanised Josh into action. He grabbed both horses' reins and calmed them down as their ears twitched at the sudden noises.

"Two more horses!" The shout echoed around the walls of the outer canyon.

"That were easy pickings!" The answering yell was followed by a loud, braying laugh, which sounded exactly like a donkey. "Funny, though, just two Indian boys on their own. Well, they ain't no more, and their losses are our gain."

Shouts and the harness jingling could be heard as horses came nearer to Josh and Amy's hiding place. Another shouted remark was followed again by the high-pitched, braying laugh echoing around the walls of the canyon. Then silence, as the horses rode off further into the canyons of the Devil's Mountain.

"That laugh!" Josh's eyes were wide with recognition. He felt his heart pumping as the realisation hit him. "I know that laugh! I remember..." And it was gone. The desperation he felt when he realised the previous snippet of memory in that moment had gone was devastating. Josh turned and buried his head in the horse's neck. "I knew that laugh! I remembered it for a second ... And then nothing more."

"That must have been the man who attacked you,"

Amy said. Josh was conscious of the enquiring look she threw at him. "Nothing else? You only remember that laugh?" She questioned him as she got on her horse.

"Nothing else!" Was Josh's disconsolate reply as he, too, climbed on his horse. They both, without a word, turned to race away towards the place where the gunfire and the screaming had been.

They could see the churned up earth that had been left by the men, and they rode on urgently, hoping to find someone alive, someone they could help.

"I thought those men had moved on. Why are they still hanging around?" Amy said.

"Didn't the sheriff say that he was certain they'd gone?" asked Josh.

"Yes, I don't understand. If they robbed a bank, why stay where they might be discovered by the local law officer?"

"What if they were working with that local law officer? What if they were friendly with Sheriff Cody?" Josh asked Amy.

Amy didn't reply. She had seen the two bodies lying on the ground. At first sight, she had thought they were bundles of rags.

Throwing herself off her horse, Amy rushed over and dropped beside the two figures. They lay sprawled out, both shot down as they ran. One was a tall, muscular Native American man who lay with several bullet wounds in his chest. His arm had been stretched out towards the smaller figure as if he was trying to reach him: a young boy who had also been shot in the chest. A blanket lay between them, and moccasins had fallen off the feet of the younger one and lay as mute witnesses to their frantic dash for escape.

Josh bent over the taller Native American man and shook his head at Amy. "It's no good. They shot him so many times, poor devil. He never stood a chance."

"This boy is ... It's a girl!" Amy had gently turned the figure over and was stunned to find the long hair falling from the delicate features of a young Native American girl. Her moccasins had fallen from her feet when she had attempted to run from the bandits. Her feet were now bloodstained as the blood poured down her leg. Blood was also pumping from the wounds in her chest. Her eyes were glazing over, but at the touch of Amy's gentle hands, she seemed to pull herself back to life.

"Save him! Care for him! Please." Her bloodstained hand was taken from the wound that she had been trying to staunch and reached out to Amy's plaited braid. The girl pulled Amy closer and whispered again. "Please, promise you'll care for him."

"I'll... I don't know..." Amy began speaking, and then became aware of crying sounds behind some rocks.

Both Amy and Josh turned to look towards the rocks. Josh jumped to his feet and rushed behind them. A baby lay swaddled in blankets.

"It's a baby. He's unharmed." Josh picked up the baby and rushed back to Amy and the Indians. He passed the tiny infant to Amy, who was still crouched down beside the dying girl.

Amy took the baby and held it closer to the mother. The dying girl stroked the cheek of the infant, who stared, wide-eyed, at its mother. Then her hand reached out to Amy's arm and clutched it with a vice-like grip. "You promise, you care for him."

"I promise you, I will care for him." Amy's words obviously reached the dying woman's last moments, because she gave a sweet smile to Amy and her son and drifted away.

Josh helped Amy to loosen the grip of the Indian woman's fingers on her arm. He took the baby from her in one hand and helped her to rise from the stiff and awkward position she had been forced to maintain beside the woman during those last moments.

"What shall we do?" Josh asked the girl. He was at a loss. A trip out treasure hunting was what he'd expected from this morning. Josh had thought it would be a fruitless journey into the foothills of the Devil's Mountain. He was convinced that this Jesuit gold search was nothing better than a pipedream of a dying man. He had gone along with it because he felt it gave the entire family a focus. While they were fixated on finding the Jesuit gold, the reality of Luke facing death was put to one side. Now, here he was, with two dead Indians at his feet and a baby in his arms. And still that memorable braying laugh rang in his ears.

"They must be part of a group. So many Indians are on the move now. The tribes have been chased out of their ancestral homes and land and are forced to move to reservations. These reservations are many miles from where they have been living for generations. Some are on poor, scrubby land which they will find hard to farm and exist upon. These Indians may be part of a group on the move. I doubt they will have been on their own. I expect others from their tribe will come looking for them. The girl spoke English so well, she was no ordinary Indian. She must also have had contact apart from her tribe." Whilst Josh stood holding the baby, Amy bent down and began straightening the bodies. "Those villains took their weapons, but that's all. Let me place the baby in the shade for now. Josh, can you help me move the Indians back into the rocks and lay them out with respect? Then we'll cover their bodies with some brush. Take care, there are no critters hiding in it."

The sparse vegetation yielded just enough to shield the bodies and keep them covered, hopefully until their tribe found them. Amy straightened their arms and hands, and after they had completed what she felt was due to them, she stood and prayed over them.

"What are you doing?" Josh asked Amy, puzzled by her new actions. She had a branch in her hand and was drawing on the rough, sandy ground.

"It's a broken horseshoe. I'm leaving a sign for our ranch. Ezra is on good terms with the local Indians and these may well know of him and the ranch. It's a sign for them to come and find the infant."

The horseshoe, with its broken piece, was an obvious sign to anyone. But Josh thought her attempt at depicting the infant was dismal. It looked like a large melon with two spots. But Amy had tried her best, and he knew he couldn't do any better. Josh also realised that he wouldn't have had the wit to think of it.

The journey back was slow and steady. It had to be. Carrying the infant on horseback was difficult, although they took it in turns. The horse's jogging motion kept the baby sleeping, but it was with relief that they drew nearer to the ranch.

Josh suddenly let out a tremendous yell of laughter, causing Amy to jump in alarm.

"What's got into you?" She said, her eyes wide, looking at him as if he had gone mad.

"What is it? What's wrong?"

# CHAPTER TWENTY-TWO

"Three!" The laughter bubbled up within him. "Remember, I told you that everything goes in threes. This baby is the third stray soul that you have brought back to the ranch. I was the first, Chan was the second, and now this Indian baby. I can't wait to see your Pa's face!" Josh threw back his head, the blonde hair flopping wildly, and gave a laugh that made his horse flick its ears in alarm.

Amy sulked the entire way back. Josh realised she was actually worried this time about the reaction of her father. He knew her father was a good Christian who would take the infant into their home and make it welcome. But this child was yet another mouth to feed. Amy's excursions were to make money by finding gold, not to increase the family's burden by finding strays needing their help.

The explanations were brief because the baby cried when the soothing horse ride ended.

Although the infant was tiny, its bawling, indignant cries were certainly not. The tiny homestead seemed to shake with the noise and no one could speak over it.

"That's not crying!" Ben said, placing his hands over his ears. "That's bawling! Make it stop, Amy. Can't you make it stop?"

They stood in a circle around the baby that had been placed on the table. Furiously angry at the disruption of its routine and extremely hungry, the child screamed and cried. It was Leah who took charge. The door was thrust open, and she stomped in to glare at every one of them. The wiry, grey-haired wife of Ezra had always been a soft-spoken woman who usually deferred to her husband. She preferred to stay out of the limelight and let him take centre stage. Not today! Leah began by issuing orders. "Luke, boil some water. Amy, find a glass jar or bottle and a clean, white rag. Ezra, you go back to our cabin and find the jug of milk on the cool slab. Bring it here."

Allotted their tasks, her minions rushed about, not one of them daring to deviate from her instructions. The hot water was used to clean the glass jar and the already clean cloth. Amy watched these operations carried out with precision by Leah. While the older woman was preparing a feed for the baby, Amy walked up and down the room, trying to calm the crying infant. She had little success, as the angry yells continued to erupt from the tiny frame and the chubby fists waved in the air with hungry desperation.

"Leah, how do you know how to do all this?" It was Ben who asked the question. It had been on all of their minds as they watched the old woman. Only Ben had been tactless enough to ask the question.

"Had one of my own, didn't I? Another lusty boy like this one. I was taught to do this by a clever medical woman when we lived back East," was her answer.

Silence greeted this remark. Everyone wanted to know what had happened to the boy. Not one of them dared to ask, not even Ben had the courage to frame a question. Ezra said nothing. He stood holding the jug of milk, his eyes lowered as he watched his wife carry out her tasks.

Leah continued speaking. She must have known what they were all wondering. "Went off to the war. He went off to be a soldier, and that's the last we saw of him." There was a finality in those words that ended the conversation.

Dipping the cloth into the milk, Leah bent over the child and placed it into the tiny mouth. The child tried to spit it out at first, then began sucking on it. The silence from him was like a blow to their senses as it enfolded them, but the echoes of his howls still rang in their ears. After that, the child slept. Leah found a wicker basket, and in this they made the child comfortable after swaddling it in another blanket. Amy could not stop the tears that ran from her eyes as she wiped, with a damp cloth, the bloodstained fingerprints of the baby's mother from its cheek. It seemed so wrong to wipe away those last remnants of his mother's love.

"I'll watch over him during the night. At my age, sleep is hard to come by. You need your rest, Amy, as does your father. With the lungs on this little one, he'd soon have you all awake!" Amy followed Leah with the baby. Both women set the basket down beside Leah's bed, so that she would be at hand when the child awoke.

"I brought the baby home. I should look after it," said Amy. She was standing at the door of Leah's home. "I feel I'm putting you to such a lot of trouble."

"Nonsense, I've known how to look after babies before this," was Leah's gruff reply.

The sun was setting, dropping lower in the sky. Josh stood on the porch, his hands on the porch rail. He'd been here for a few days now, but never failed to come out on the porch each evening. It had been a few days now since that first sunset. But the awesome spectacle had got into his soul, and now each evening he had to come and watch it as if it had been the very first time. The open landscape, stretching as far as one could see, lay out in front of him. The sky was wide and enormous. Josh knew he had never seen such a wonderful expanse as that which lay before him. Again, this knowledge, coming from somewhere in the back of his brain, left him furious and frustrated. The colours of gold, red, and orange lit up the earth with a rosy tinge.

The saguaro cacti stood tall and forbidding. Their shadows, long and dark, stretched across the open ground, seeming to move and become alive at this time of day. When Josh turned to look behind the ranch, he saw the peaks of the Devil's Mountain jutting into the sky. The flat-topped hills to one side also glowed, from the diminishing sun's rays, with a myriad colours on the rocks, shrubby patches, and the many cacti of different shapes, along with their dark purple shadows. Forbidding as the peaks of the Devil's Mountain were in daytime, the sunset colours changed them. Vibrant tones vied with the darkest of sombre hues in crevasses and canyons which promised intriguing avenues of treasure-hunting exploration.

When Josh looked at them, he readily understood Amy's fear of being caught out in those mountains when darkness fell.

Josh never saw them arrive. One moment he was watching the sunset, the next moment the ranch was surrounded. Statue-like, they sat on their horses, immobile. Even their horses neither swished their tails nor stamped their hooves.

# CHAPTER TWENTY-THREE

The Indians on horseback, were watching and waiting. Josh swallowed hard. Their eerie and uncanny appearance had shaken him. He struggled to find his voice, but it came out as a squeaky whisper. He called out to Luke, Ezra, and Ben, who ran out to join him on the porch. Standing beside him, they were also stunned and silent. Leah came from the cabin and brought the baby with her. She and Amy stood on the porch steps. The Indians sat on their horses, motionless, gazing at the silent, frightened group.

"Don't reach for a weapon. They could kill each one of us in an instant if they wanted to. Think they would have killed us by now if they had planned to. Best wait to see what it is they've come for." Ezra's whisper sounded loud in the silence. Still, the Indians sat astride their horses, watching and waiting.

Amy turned towards Leah. The girl took the baby from the older woman's arms. Both she and Leah had taken turns in dipping the rag in the milk, urging the little one to suck from it. Softly snuffling, he was content and happy. Leah straightened the blanket around the infant and helped Amy down the steps.

Josh put out a hand to halt Amy's progress, but Ezra grabbed his hand and whispered to him. "Leave her, Josh. They only want the child."

Josh watched the girl and the baby as they walked slowly towards the Indians. He wanted to run after her, grab her, and bring her back to the safety of the cabin. But that was nonsense. Not one of them was safe with the Indians stationed around the property. The Indians could attack them and it would all be over in an instant, and none of them could survive an attack by this many. Josh's fists were clenched tight as he watched the girl approach the tall, mounted Indian. Her courage in the face of so many of them was amazing. If ever he had admired the girl, that admiration had increased tenfold this night.

The tall, commanding figure, with a decided air of authority, rode forward. His horse stopped beside Amy as she stood beneath the sign of the Broken Horseshoe Ranch. The man was obviously the leader of this tribe of Indians. He looked down at the infant and Amy holding him in her arms.

"You covered their bodies?" His voice rang out. The question hung in the air as the setting sun made his shadow loom large over the girl and infant. "Why?"

"I tried to protect them from scavengers and out of respect. I knew someone would come for them," Amy answered him. Her voice was clear and calm, despite the stress and strain she was under. In the fading light of the sun, she stood tall, and the clear voice with its tension obvious to Josh seemed to touch something in his heart.

"Why did you take the child?" The question seemed important to the man.

"She asked me to. His mother asked me to care for him," was Amy's reply. Again, her voice was clear, only the slightest of tremors betraying her fear.

"She lived?" The harsh question was barked out at the girl. The Indian leader seemed surprised at this and eager to find out more.

"A moment only. She asked me to care for him. I've given him some cow's milk, and he's quiet now. I promised her I would care for her child."

The silence seemed to stretch for hours. The group standing silently on the porch watched helplessly as Amy held the focus of all those eyes. Still, the Indians standing sentinel around the ranch didn't move, except for their heads. They centred all eyes upon Amy and the infant. Then, the chief gave a signal and a young woman rode up beside him, jumped down, and went towards Amy. She took the child from Amy's arms, looked down at it, and smiled. A glance upwards to the chief, a few whispered words, and she looked towards Amy. The Indian woman took a step towards the girl and Josh felt himself stiffen. Her hand reached up to the girl and gently stroked Amy's cheek. Then the Indian woman had leapt up onto her horse, still with the baby, and re-joined the group that was behind the chief.

"You have cared for the child as if it were your own, she tells me. It will be remembered."

Again, the chief gave another hand signal. A young man dropped off his horse and, reaching for his axe, walked towards Amy.

# CHAPTER TWENTY-FOUR

The Indian walked past Amy towards the gatepost. His glance flicked over her. The axe was raised, and he hacked out a symbol in the wood before walking back past Amy, again with that fleeting glance towards the girl. Leaping astride his horse, he and the entire group wheeled round and vanished in a cloud of dust. The rising dust became an orange trail behind them as the very last ray of the sun lit the departing Indians. For a long moment, they all watched that trail disappear into the black shadows of the Devil's Mountain.

Luke walked into the cabin and called out to them. "We need a drink." The tiniest tots of whiskey were eked out to each one of them, but Ben and Chan were given coffee instead. There was silence as each one of them digested the experience that they had all gone through. Death at the hands of Indians was something they all feared. And, during that strange time, when facing those Indians, death seemed to be imminent.

It was Ezra who spoke first. "Don't know what tribe they were. There were no tribal feathers or markings upon them." He slurped the whiskey from his tin mug, rolling it over his tongue.

"Weren't they the Indians that you are friendly with, Ezra?" Luke queried the older man. Luke's face was gaunt and his voice was weak. The stress of seeing his daughter face a tribe of Indians had left the sick man exhausted. It was taking all his strength to lift the tin mug with the whiskey to his mouth.

Ezra shook his head, and the long white locks moved erratically. "No, I know a few that live on the other side of Nowhere. Think that they are probably Crow. This lot looks as if they're trying to keep out of trouble by hiding their tribal markings and clothes."

"Why did they make that sign on the gatepost?" Ben asked Ezra. "Chan and I've been up to look at it. It just looks like a squiggle to me. What do you think it means?"

"Had a look at it myself. Don't know Indian signs. But I reckon that they have put us under their protection. We've got you to thank for that, Amy girl. Reckon you did a good thing after all, bringing the baby back home. He was something special, that baby. I reckon he was the Chief's son." Ezra's words were said in a quiet, thoughtful manner, so unlike his usual pattern of speech. The older man had been terrified just as much as the rest of them. Relief and that tiny tot of whiskey had loosened his thoughts into speech.

Again, there was silence in the cabin. Each single one of them had to come to terms with this experience they had gone through in their own way. They had faced Indians that outnumbered them and had surrounded their cabin. They all thought they were going to be massacred. The overwhelming relief at being left unharmed was still being absorbed.

"Why did those bank robber guys kill those Indians? There were only two of them," Ben asked Ezra.

"For the sport, I reckon! Mean varmints like them would do that sort of thing," muttered Ezra.

Leah placed her tin mug, now emptied of whiskey, down on the table. "Why are those bank robbing men still here? That sheriff said they were long gone. Why are they still around our land?" Leah's questions had everyone's attention.

"Do you think the sheriff and those men...?" Ben began putting into words what they were all thinking.

"Yes, Ben, I think there's something fishy about that sheriff. Seems as if he may well be in cahoots with those guys. Maybe he's getting a share of their money. Never liked the man, wouldn't put anything past him." Ezra took another sip of the whiskey. The frightening experience and the whiskey were turning Ezra into a talker!

"I don't understand how that Indian chief, and the poor woman who was killed, spoke such good English?" Amy asked Ezra.

"You got me there, girl! Strange that, never knew Indians so well spoken, and that's a fact. Real puzzle there," Ezra said as he finished the last of his whiskey with a lick of his lips.

The Widow Perkins arrived the next morning with her entire workforce. "Call me 'Nancy'," she said when she arrived. "Don't think I will ever get used to being called Mrs Tanner. 'Nancy' is good enough for me!" The Mexican family that lived with her on Dry Creek Ranch and the two disabled soldiers that had wandered onto the ranch one day for a meal and had never left came with her.

"This here is Miguel, his wife, and their sons, and my two soldier guys, Bill and Nat. Good workers, all of them, glad to come over and give a hand. Well, apart from Bill, he's lost one hand. He won't give you another, that one's all he's got!" Nancy roared with laughter at her joke and Josh was relieved to see that Bill was quite happy to enjoy the joke as well.

The ex-soldiers were both remnants of the armies that roamed the country after the Civil War. No one knew, or wanted to know, which side they'd fought on. It was best left that way. One had lost a hand, the other a leg. They had fought bravely, and that's all folks needed to know. They put in some work as best they could, which was all that mattered. Taken in by the Widow, they had found a home and a purpose to their lives on Dry Creek Ranch.

"We've come to build on that extra room you need. I've brought over some timber. I brought over more of my animals. You've got my cow, so that Luke can have the milk and butter to build up his strength. Now I've seen the water you have and the good grazing, I brought more of my livestock. This way, we can both help each other out. Gonna work out well, I can see that." Nancy stood, her hands on her hips, and grinned at them all.

An overpowering woman with a voice like a foghorn, but Josh realised Nancy had a heart of gold and was someone he would be proud to call a friend. He wasn't so sure afterwards when he was also set to work by her. The sweat poured off him and it wasn't until he got sympathetic smiles from her usual workforce that he realised that this was Nancy's way of getting them all going. A hard taskmaster she may be, but she made them stop for a rest and drink and did not expect them to do more than they were capable of.

Josh had noticed Ben was always scribbling into a notebook. He walked over to the boy, looking over Ben's shoulder as the words seemed to flow from his pencil. The boy's eyes were wide with interest as he watched the animals being untethered from the buggy and led out onto the good grass. "You writing again?" Josh asked the boy.

"Yes, I take notes and then write it all up later," was Ben's reply. "Don't let Pa or Amy find out what I'm doing."

"And what exactly are you doing, Ben?" Josh asked the boy.

# CHAPTER TWENTY-FIVE

Looking about him, making certain that he was out of earshot of his father and sister, Ben whispered. "That letter you posted for me."

"Why was it such a secret? I don't like keeping secrets from your father and Amy. Why shouldn't they know about it?" Josh asked Ben. "Was it to a girl back home, sweetheart, maybe?"

"No! I haven't got a stupid girlfriend. It's going to a newspaper. They carry articles about the Wild West, the gold rush and suchlike. I've seen some pieces written about the Cattle Drives and building the railroads. I thought maybe I could sell articles about living here in the foothills of the Devil's Mountain."

"Well done, Ben. It's a great idea, and I wish you luck with it!" was Josh's enthusiastic reply.

Ben smiled at Josh. His eyes were wide with excitement and his freckles almost dancing with pleasure at sharing his secret with a supportive ally. "It was my English teacher. He knew our circumstances and my love of writing, and he helped me all the time. Before we left, he gave me the address and name of a newspaperman to contact. He thought I could earn money with my scribbles!"

"It's well worth trying. Maybe you will earn money, Ben. I'll post anything else for you." Josh smiled at the boy as Ben wandered away, notebook in hand.

It was lunchtime. Leah brought from her kitchen a gigantic pot of chilli. If there were more beans in it and only a little meat from a couple of rabbits Ezra had caught, no one said anything. Cornbread added to their meal, and they sat round on the porch and on the steps, eating hungrily.

"I'm amazed, Nancy, how fast you have all got on. That lumber you brought over has nearly done that entire room. You've all worked well and I can see we're going to have a new room for our visitor." Luke beamed at the assembled group.

Josh thought he was the only one who saw the peculiar expression flit across Nancy's face. What was she up to? That room was quite large and had gone up with an amazing speed. He thought there was more to Nancy and her kindness to those at Broken Horseshoe Ranch.

Amy, sitting on the bottom step of the porch, was startled when Nancy dropped down beside her. "Luke is looking better recently, isn't he? Since I brought that cow over, and he's been having milk and some butter, I think he's filling out some."

"Yes, he is! I can't thank you enough, Nancy. The milk and the fresh eggs from the chickens have helped Pa enormously." Amy's reply showed her gratitude and her relief that her father was improving slightly. Maybe, just maybe, that doctor had been right after all, thought Josh, as he sat beside them. Josh, overhearing the conversation, could see that the entry into the Tanner's life of Widow Perkins was proving to be a force to the good.

"Well, girl, you graze my animals on your better land. You get the products."

Laughter erupted between the Mexicans, the ex-soldiers, and Luke and Ezra. Josh smiled with the others, unsure of what the joke was, but pleased to join in with that happy moment.

"A rider! Someone is coming!" Ben, ever watchful, was the first to spot the figure riding towards the ranch. "It's the sheriff!"

The laughter faded away and an uneasy silence crept over the group as the sheriff rode up to the ranch.

"What a merry group you all are! Aren't you? Widow Perkins, you pulled a fast one on me. Or you thought you did! Laugh all you want now. Not one of you will be laughing before this day is out!"

# CHAPTER TWENTY-SIX

"I ain't Widow Perkins no more. I'm Mrs Tanner now." Nancy stood facing the sheriff with her hands on her ample hips and her messy bun escaping its confines as she shook her head. Tendrils of hair escaped and hung down her back as she faced the man with defiance.

The sheriff cast her a look of intense dislike, almost of hatred. "Married the sick man, didn't you? Now you got yourself Broken Horseshoe Ranch and your own property. Heard that you've willed the Dry Creek Ranch to those two young ones. The preacher fellow has been spreading the news all over town."

"It's my ranch! I can will it to who I please, and I can marry who I want to," was the angry answer from Nancy. She gestured to Ben and Amy, who were now standing beside her. "They're both my family now. They're my stepchildren!"

The sheriff sat on his horse. It was a large, rangy animal, powerful enough to bear his weight. He gave them a slow smile, which made Josh's blood run cold. This man was pure evil. There was no way that this confrontation was going to end without bloodshed. Josh could only watch and wait for the sheriff to make the next move.

"I have a fancy to be the owner of the Dry Creek Ranch and the Broken Horseshoe Ranch. That would suit me real fine." He settled back onto his horse, somehow making himself look more at ease. The confident, ringing tones in his voice set off alarm bells in Josh. There was a glib assurance in this man's manner that worried him.

"Yes, I shall be the owner of both ranches. You did me a favour willing Dry Creek Ranch to these young ones."

For such a heavy man, he jumped lightly down from his horse and took out his gun. He pointed it at Amy and walked up the porch steps and grabbed her by the arm, pulling her close to him. "Yes, I have a mind to marry this one and that way I'll inherit both ranches. Yes, I want both ranches and I'm going to have them! Your will makes that so easy for me, my dear Nancy. You will all be dead, except for Amy." A tongue came out, licking the lips of the sheriff's fleshy face, his deep-set, hooded eyes glittering as they ranged up and down the girl's body, taking in every detail. "Amy will be my wife. I'll let her live, and then I can own both ranches."

"Leave her be!" said Josh, and made as if to grab Amy.

"Oh no! You don't tell me what to do!" The lightning fast move from the sheriff took them all unawares. His hand, holding the gun, swept across Josh's face, knocking him off the porch and onto the ground. "You all do as I say, when I say." He stepped down and kicked Josh, who was attempting to get to his feet. That kick sent him back down with a groan as the sheriff's boot connected with his wounded back.

Amy screamed and would have run down to Josh but for the vice-like grip on her arm. She struggled again, but in vain. The man was so powerful, with enormous strength.

"Leave my daughter alone. Sheriff, you must have gone mad. No lawman should behave this way. Please let my daughter go. Leave my ranch immediately and none of us will say anything more about this." Luke's carefully measured tones only made the man laugh.

The enormous beer belly wobbled as he laughed uproariously. "None of you will say anything about it! You're right there, because you will all be dead. Those nasty bank robbing guys have come around and shot you all. Except for this pretty little girl! I've a fancy for this young one."

Amy struggled in his grip, trying to kick him and pull away from him. "I won't marry you! I wouldn't marry you if you were the last man on earth!" The disgust she felt for the man rang out in her voice.

The eyes of the man holding her narrowed. Her obvious disgust of him enraged him. The sheriff's face changed into a mask of hatred and he flung her away from him, hurling her onto the dirt off the porch steps. Josh, who had by this time risen to his feet, bent down and pulled Amy up, and held her close to him with an arm around her.

"If you don't marry me, you can die like the rest of them," the man snarled at Amy.

"Riders! More riders, and they're coming this way," Ben shouted, pointing towards the low cliffs that were the beginning of the foothills of the Devil's Mountain. Three men rode across the pasture and the rough ground towards the ranch at speed.

The sheriff smiled and waved a hand to the three riders, who drew nearer to him. They were spread out in a long line. One, drawing nearer to the sheriff, yelled at him. "Got your message, Sheriff! Here we are. What little job have you got in mind for us this time?" He gave a loud braying laugh, exactly like a donkey.

Josh stiffened and stared at the man. Black hair hung down in greasy locks beneath the old hat clamped upon his head. The dark, glittering eyes wandered over each one of them with malicious intent. A hooked nose, out of shape after a few breaks, roamed over his face. "What job you got in mind for us, Sheriff?" he repeated. Again he laughed. That laugh made Josh tingle with recognition. This man he knew! That laugh he'd heard before. As the man gazed from one to the other, the dismissive glance at Josh showed he didn't remember Josh at all.

"That's the man who killed the Indians. I recognise that laugh," whispered Amy into Josh's ear.

"Yes, you're right," he replied.

"This little job you're going to do for me is to kill these folks. The poor souls are going to be murdered by those wicked bank robbers who were passing through." The sheriff gave a deep laugh as he said this, his belly flapping over his belt buckle in time with his guffaws. The second rider was almost upon them, but the third rider was still a little way behind.

Josh looked at the latecomer and thought he saw movement behind him in the spindly vegetation.

# CHAPTER TWENTY-SEVEN

Josh looked harder at the rocks and spindly vegetation beside the trail that the last rider was following to the ranch. He raised his hand to shield his eyes from the glare of the sun. Was that a flash? There was definitely a movement behind a rock, and he caught sight of a figure. Almost immediately, that rider fell silently from his horse to land on the ground, looking like a bundle of rags. The rags twitched for a moment and then lay still. The horse careered onwards, keen to join his companions.

Again, almost imperceptibly, Josh was aware of further movements behind rocks and saw figures moving along the narrow gullies left by the rains. Even the spindly brush seemed alive. A dusky hand appeared behind a rock with a bow. The arrow flew silently from it to pierce the back of the second cowboy. He, too, fell from his horse. The man with the hooked nose heard the thump that the second man had made when he landed, his horse rearing and neighing in alarm at the sudden loss of his rider. Hooked nose opened his mouth to call out to the sheriff, but he never spoke. He never, ever gave that braying donkey laugh again. This arrow hit him in the neck and he, too, fell from his horse.

The group standing in front of the Broken Horseshoe Ranch was silent. Fear and horror at the sheriff's arrival and his threats towards them had them focused entirely upon him. It was only Josh who was aware of the ongoing drama behind the sheriff. Unaware of the loss of his fellow evildoers, the sheriff bent forward to draw out his rifle, but his hand never reached it. His fall onto the ground was much louder than the other cowboys'. His bulk hit the ground with an almighty splat and the dust rose around it, settling with a sigh beside him.

A wild whoop of triumph echoed around the ranch itself and reverberated from the hills and jagged peaks beyond. Indians rose from their shallow, dusty hiding places and were joined by others who came leading their horses. One figure stood tall on his horse and gave the party a salute. A final war cry came from him, and the others followed his wild gallop across the rocky ground to disappear again into the foothills and canyons of the Devil's Mountain.

Amy suddenly sat on the ground. Josh realised that her legs no longer supported her. Luke and Nancy sank down onto a porch step. The Mexican family clung to their mother, who had prayed constantly during the ordeal in muttered whispers, only the *clack, clack* of her rosary beads being her constant accompaniment. Now her prayers of thanksgiving were shouted in joy, and every single one of them joined her family to shout "Amen" with her.

It was Nancy! Of course, it had to be Nancy who organised them, Josh thought. She stood up, her hands again on those ample hips, preparatory to her announcement. "Does anyone want to take these varmints and the sheriff into town and explain what has happened?"

There was no answer. Not one person thought of a reply.

"Thought so!" Nancy then grabbed Ezra by the arm. "Do you know where Hell's Mouth Canyon is?"

The old man smiled at her, then his broad, gummy grin widened and he nodded at her. He glanced over at Luke. "This old girl got a good brain on her! Done got yourself a fine wife here, Luke!"

Josh swallowed a grin as he saw the blush mingled with the look of abject terror cross Luke's face as a realisation of what and whom he had married finally hit him.

"Yes, Nancy, you got it right here. No need to kick up dust about that evil bag of lard and his robber pals. Don't want a crowd chasing after them Indians either. Those Indians got their revenge for the murder of their two young ones. They saved our lives at the same time. Got to respect that," Ezra said.

There was a general agreement from everyone at this, and Nancy nodded. "Let's get rid of these bodies and forget we ever saw these guys. Everyone okay with that?"

Josh was nervous. He didn't like the sound of the journey up through those mountains. Josh did not like heights. Most of all, he didn't like the sound of Hell's Mouth Canyon.

# CHAPTER TWENTY-EIGHT

Before they left the ranch, they had the unpleasant task of collecting the bodies. "Let's get them sorted out in front of the ranch first, before we load them on the horses," Ezra had said. "The guns and ammunition should be shared out between us all."

Amy stood looking down with horror at the bodies, and the guns, ammunition, and knives that lay beside them. For so few men, there were so many weapons. "They have loads of weapons between them. Their main purpose in life was killing, wasn't it?" Amy asked Josh, her brown eyes filling with tears as she remembered the broken bodies of the two young Indians. Her small, sunburnt hand wiped away the tears from her brown eyes.

"Yes, they were downright evil and deserved to die. I'm glad we didn't have to kill them though, and I'm grateful the Indians did it for us," Josh said.

Nancy stomped over to join them. "Josh, you never spoke a truer word! I was always suspicious of the sheriff but never did I think he was that mean and ornery." She shook her head, the white hair coming loose again. Her grimace of distaste was felt both by Amy and Josh.

Luke walked over to join the group. "They were killers right enough, but they were God's children, and I reckon it wouldn't go amiss if we said a prayer for their eternal souls. Bow your heads and we'll pray."

They all did as he told them, but Josh knew it went hard against his feelings to pray for such as those who lay before him: dead through their own evil actions. Luke was a true God-fearing man, so Josh said a prayer in his mind. If it wasn't a wholehearted prayer, that was between him and his maker.

"Those Indians saved our lives. If you're all agreeable, I suggest we leave a couple of horses and some blankets and jackets for them. The guns we keep ourselves, I don't want any guns in the hands of Indians," Nancy said.

"That huge horse of the sheriff's is well known in these parts, that one must definitely go to the Indians. We don't want to be seen with it or questions may be asked," Ezra said as he got the sheriff's body ready to be slung over that horse.

"One of my piglets can also go with us to leave for them. Another gift thanking them for our deliverance." Nancy looked around at them, as if expecting an argument, but no one could quibble with that.

It was a long, circuitous ride up winding, steep cliffs. Josh discovered that his dislike for heights had now turned into an active hatred. With his eyes firmly fixed on Amy's back as she rode before him, somehow he coped. He had taken a couple of glances down to the valley floor far beneath them, but that had left him feeling sick and dizzy. It was colder the further they went up the mountains, but Josh was sweating and his constant fear threatened to overwhelm him at times.

Just when he thought he had reached his limit and could go no further and would have to confess to the others to his eternal shame, they navigated the narrowest ledge of all to find Hell's Mouth Canyon. Over that ledge and dropping down was a black hole of nothingness. It took everything Josh had in courage to help heave and roll those bodies down the cliff's face.

After the bodies had tumbled away into oblivion, they began the descent.

"Are you all right, Josh? You don't like heights, do you?" Amy asked as they climbed back onto their horses.

The other riderless horses they were leading back down, now considerably lighter without their burdens of the dead men.

Josh brushed his long, blonde hair back from his forehead and stared at the concerned face of Amy. Her interest in and consideration for everyone around her was endearing. But he could have wished that she hadn't realised how he had been affected by this journey up the steep cliffs.

"I'll be all right. Surely the worst is over. We reached the top and now we descend to the valley." He gave her a forced smile.

"If you get bad, just shout out and we can stop for a moment. Your horse knows the way and will take care. Only look at the path in front of you, not the valley below," Amy told him as they mounted up and set off on the homeward journey.

Halfway home, Ezra called upon them to halt. They dismounted and stood beside their horses, sipping water and unpacking the gifts they had brought for the Indians. Josh's legs held him when he dismounted from his horse, but only just. The journey down the steep cliff ledges had been far worse than the journey up. The constant need to look ahead meant, as he negotiated the narrow bends, his eyes unwittingly fell upon the land so far below.

"You did it, Josh! Well done. I know how hard it was for you."

Amy's sympathetic pat on his arm meant so much to Josh. He was surprised at the gratitude he felt towards this young woman.

On the journey, both from the ranch and now on the way back, they had known that the Indians were watching them. There had been movements in the brush, behind rocks, and even the cacti did not completely hide the Indians from view. Together, they unloaded the gifts they had brought for the Indians: the two horses, blankets, jackets, and bedrolls and, of course, the piglet. They were piled up, the horses and the piglet tied to the spindly branches of a tree.

It was Amy who called out to the Indians. Her clear, youthful voice echoed across the plain and bounced from the rocks. "Thank you. You saved our lives. We leave these gifts for you. The dead have gone. No one will ever know you've been here. Thank you."

Josh brought up the rear of the party, and it was Josh who looked behind as they reached a bend in the trail. The Indians were rummaging through the gifts. The Chief saw Josh looking back, and he raised a hand in salute. Josh did likewise, and rode on, following the others back to Broken Horseshoe Ranch.

They were nearly home. Amy was talking to Nancy, and Ezra was leading the way with two of the horses behind him. Josh, recovering from his dreadful height experience, was still mulling over thoughts of the man and his braying laugh. If only the man had lived, even for a short time. If only Josh could have found out where the man had found him and where his belongings were. Maybe they could find them. Perhaps they could find the bank robbers' hideout, Josh thought.

# CHAPTER TWENTY-NINE

Amy turned round on her horse and shouted at Josh. "Soon be home! Won't be long now." Josh waved back and smiled at her enthusiasm to reach the ranch. Nancy was riding alongside Amy, the bulky woman astride her horse with her usual competence. They had both drawn ahead of Ezra and Josh. Both women were deep in conversation. Josh thought it was doing Amy good to have another woman to keep her company. How she must've missed her mother when she died, leaving her alone to cope with her sick father and younger brother.

Home? This was Amy's home. She had shouted home to him as if she thought it was now his home. Was it his home as well? Did Amy expect him to stay and make it his permanent home?

"Be glad to get back for a rest. Getting too old for these shenanigans," said Ezra.

"You will never be too old for any shenanigans!" laughed Josh.

The old man smiled in delight at this remark, and they rode on in a companionable silence.

The scenery around Josh was now familiar to him. Several times he had ridden this way. There was a huge rock that looked like a giant finger pointing up to the sky, the group of tiny cactus plants clustered in a group together. They were round balls of spikes, lethal if you got near to them. A twisted branch of a tree that was weathered by the sun and wind. Josh knew without looking that they were coming close to the whitened bones and skulls of some animals left lying after they had been devoured by predators.

"Still no memory, Josh?" Ezra's voice broke into

Josh's thoughts. "Been sometime since that blow on the head. Thought maybe you'd remembered something by now."

"Nothing, Ezra, and I'm worried now that I will never remember anything! This might be all I know about myself. The words written on a scrap of paper, 'Josh Barnes, go to Broken Horseshoe Ranch'," was Josh's bitter reply.

"Maybe it's for the best," the old man said, pushing his white hair, blowing in the wind, back from his face.

"Why would it be for the best, Ezra?"

"You could be a criminal, could be on the run, or escaping from an angry wife. Best not to remember if it was any of those!" was Ezra's blunt reply.

"They're coming, Pa! They're coming," Ben's voice greeted them as they drew near to the ranch. Ben was waving his hat, Chan was waving both arms in the air. The Chinese boy had been lucky, the dislocation of his arm had not been too severe.

Josh looked at the familiar sight, these people that he'd got to know so well. Josh was interested in Ben, eager to help his attempted journalism dreams. He, too, was worried about Luke's health and his problems. Somehow, they had become his own. If he really admitted to himself, it was Amy that was the major draw that kept him at Broken Horseshoe Ranch. He'd admitted it finally to himself, but to no one else. He couldn't, not until he knew who he was and why he was riding to this ranch.

Tomorrow, he and Amy would search for Jesuit gold as usual. Josh was going to conduct another search at the same time. Finding the bank robbers and their belongings was of the utmost importance to Josh. Those belongings may well have the evidence to tell him who he really was and why he was travelling the Devil's Mountain. But Josh had a niggling fear that perhaps he would be better off not knowing the truth!

# CHAPTER THIRTY

The search for Jesuit gold had to be postponed. Provisions were needed, and urgently. Nancy had been using up all the stores that Broken Horseshoe Ranch possessed. Both Josh and Amy set off to Nowhere to fulfil the list, the very long list, that they had been given by Nancy.

"I was looking forward to another search," said Amy, as they trundled their way along the dirt track.

"Just as it seemed we might get close to the gold, we have to get provisions for Nancy. Never mind, Amy. Let's leave very early in the morning, at dawn. That will give us plenty of time in the cool of the morning to search."

With this resolved between them, they both entered the general store with the long list.

"He killed my skillet!" Amy had been hurtled back by the gunshots. One bullet grazed her arm, which bled profusely, the other hit the middle of the skillet that she had just paid for. She lay crumpled against sacks of beans, flour, and potatoes, on the wooden floor of the general store in the town of Nowhere.

"It's old Gabe! The gold prospector! He's gone mad. I see him shooting a gun and a rifle at everything and everyone. Gabe's riding up and down Main Street, just shooting and shouting!" Manuel was peering round the door of the general store at the mayhem out in the dusty road in front of the store.

Shattered glass from the gunshots had fallen and smashed around Josh, the tinkling sound continuing as the last shards fell from the window frame.

"Amy! You've been shot! You're bleeding. Lie still and let me..." Josh flung himself down on his knees beside the girl. Aghast, he could only stare down at the blood on the white freckled face of the young woman as she lay there, her braids undone and her auburn hair loose. Her faded check shirt was splattered with blood from the wound in her arm, and her canvas skirt was covered in dust from the flour bin that she had knocked over. Josh himself had been unhurt. Not even the flying glass had injured him.

"Move out of the way! Let me see to the girl," said the store owner's wife, Eliza. She pushed Josh to one side. Her round moon face was creased in consternation as she rushed to the fallen girl. "Oh my! The poor little one! Where is all the blood coming from?" Eliza sank back on her knees, staring down at Amy. The brown pigtails Amy always wore lay tumbled loose onto the floor where she had collapsed in a heap. The freckles splashed across her face stood out against the increasingly white pallor of the injured girl. Eliza crossed herself, and putting both hands together, gazed up through the wooden ceiling. "It's a miracle! That bullet was going straight to your heart, but my skillet saved you." The excited woman took the skillet from Amy's shaking hands and held it up for all to see. "The bullet! It hit the skillet and saved her life. It's a miracle! The only blood was splashed from your arm when you fell."

Amy pushed herself up on one elbow and looked at the skillet that was being waved about in the air by Eliza. She had been choosing one to replace the old worn out one at the ranch. Then Amy looked down at her arm. Blood was pooling out of the flesh wound above her elbow. Her fall backwards onto the floor had been caused by the force of the bullet as it hit the skillet.

"That skillet! It saved your life. Amy, do you know

how near to death you came?" Josh could only wonder at the bullet deeply embedded in the metal pan. His agitation was reflected in the harsh tones of his voice. His blonde hair flopped down over his face, and, as usual, he tossed it back with an impatient hand. A tall, well-built man, he knelt beside the injured girl. Josh's blue eyes held increasing concern as he saw the blood flow from Amy's arm.

"I've only just bought it!" Amy said and tried to smile.

"Your arm, I fetch stuff to help. A bullet grazed it. Some blood, but it's not serious." Eliza patted Amy on her good arm and smiled down at the girl. A buxom, good-hearted woman, she was the ideal partner to Manuel, who ran the general store. It seemed no time at all before she arrived back and Amy's arm was washed and bound up, ready for the homeward journey.

Josh got up and stood beside Amy to ensure that she did not faint or collapse when she rose to her feet. He watched her closely, her little snub nose wrinkling as she looked down at the skillet that Eliza had placed in her hands. Manuel's voice could be heard by those inside the store as he shouted up and down the main street of the town of Nowhere. They all rushed to the door to see what was causing the commotion.

"What have you done, Gabe? You nearly killed Amy Tanner! Gabe, you've been shooting up my store! Who's going to pay for my window glass?"

A voice shouted back. "That old Gabe, the old man's gone crazy. This time he's really done it. He's looking for the sheriff, says his mine and his camp are being attacked. Says that some villains are after his gold. If the sheriff doesn't do something, he says he's going to do his job for him!"

On coming outside to see what was going on, Josh and Amy could hear Manuel shouting again. "Gabe? I want a word with you. You can give me some of your gold to pay for this window. Where are you? I want a word with you!"

# CHAPTER THIRTY-ONE

Manuel could be seen running down the street towards the old man. Gabe was sitting on a mule, waving a rifle in the air and threatening to shoot anyone that came near to him. Gabe was leading another mule laden down with bags. "I'll kill anyone who tries to steal my gold. The Thunder God has told me it's mine! Anyone tries to get it from me, the Thunder God will kill them! I'm warning everyone, it's my goldmine!"

Gabe began shooting again from the rifle, firing wildly as he wheeled around on the mule. Folk took cover, hiding behind buggies and horses, or diving into the nearest shop or building. Still waving the rifle, he rode towards them, heading out of the town. "It's my gold! The Thunder God told me it's mine! Anyone comes near me or my goldmine will perish!" He fired another shot for good measure from a pistol.

Josh pushed Amy and Eliza back into the store, fearful of the old man and his rifle. Gabe rode past them, ignoring Manuel's frantic cries for recompense of his window. Josh looked at the old man and saw his eyes were wide open with a frantic, wild look within them. Well worn and tattered clothes with many brown stains hung upon the skeleton bones of the old man. The gun was now in a holster, and Josh glimpsed a large knife thrust into the old man's belt.

"He's a wild man now! The mountains have claimed him. He belongs to them." The doom-laden tones of Eliza came from behind Josh and Amy. Both turned to look at her. "I speak the truth! That man, he is no more. The mountains have possessed him with his search for the gold. Avoid him! The Thunder God of Devil's Mountain has him tight within his grasp. Take care you do not meet Gabe again on your journeys." With a sudden movement, she grabbed Amy, giving her a kiss and a hug. "Take care, little one, take care." Then, she took Josh by the arm, and standing on tiptoe, gave him a kiss. "You're a good man. I see trouble around you, but remember always that you are a good man. You are a good man!" Eliza turned and went back into the store.

"What was that all about?" Josh asked Amy, still standing and staring after the retreating figure of Eliza.

"Eliza has feelings and visions. Sometimes she sees the future, sometimes she sees the things people should do, and sometimes she tells of actions they must not take. I've never known her wrong."

Josh felt sceptical but realised that Amy believed in Eliza's power of foretelling the future. Since finding himself adrift in this barren landscape, in a strange world of deserts, mountains, and treasure searches, Josh realised nothing was normal around him and that perhaps he should find comfort in the words of Eliza and her reassurance that he was a good man.

They had paid for the goods they'd bought before the shooting began. Amy stepped down from the boardwalk towards the buggy. Josh stood for a moment, looking up and down the main street of the town of Nowhere. This was his second visit to the town, and he found it strange to see that it seemed just the same, yet different to him. Only a few buildings were permanent, the sheriff's office and the general store having been built of solid timber. The livery stable was an old adobe building with a porch stretching a good way out from it and covering the blacksmith's forge. He remembered the saloon. The wooden front gave a false illusion, because it was inside a tent behind the front. The hotel, with its sign of beds and food, had been in another tent building. Now Josh saw that in the few days since he visited Nowhere, it had been built out of timber, and was becoming a grand structure. Josh shook his head. Nothing had been familiar on his first visit, and it still wasn't familiar. But deep within him, he knew that this land was alien to him. He'd never been here before. Funny how he knew that. Giving himself a shake, he went to join Amy at the buggy.

Amy stood by her horse. The girl was white-faced still, and the bandage round her arm was slightly red from the oozing blood. Eliza had wiped the blood from her face when she dressed the wound. It had splashed up from her arm when she fell. Amy's plaits were tousled from her fall when she had hurtled back from the force of the bullet on the skillet. But she had tidied them haphazardly, even with her injured arm. A nail-bitten hand smoothed down her skirt, brushing away the dust from the general store floor. Then she straightened the canvas jacket she always wore. Her hands shook a little as she did so, but Josh ignored it.

He came up beside her. "Are you okay to ride home now? Not too shaken up, are you?"

A smile was directed at Josh. "I'm fine, the ride will do me good," was her valiant reply.

Josh knew she felt rough and was putting on a brave face, but he followed her lead. "Let's go then, back to the ranch. We'll have a story to tell them when we get back."

"The buggy was unharmed during the shootout. Poor Bella stayed calm the whole time. Well done, Bella, you're a great girl." Amy patted the horse, grateful that their one means of transport was unhurt.

"Where is everybody? I'd have thought everyone

would be in the street. We heard enough voices shouting earlier," Josh said, looking around.

A solitary man walking down the street called to them in reply to Josh's question. "That old fool, Gabe, rode off up to those mountains after firing his rifle off, any which way. He got old Joe at the saloon in the leg and put a hole through the beer barrel. Ha! They're all in the saloon trying to mop up the beer and drink it, before it all lands on the floor."

"Are you sure you're all right to travel home?" Josh asked Amy again, as he helped her up onto the buggy.

"Yes, I'll be fine. I want Leah to have another look at this arm. She knows about wounds and has a marvellous salve that cures anything." Amy turned to wave goodbye to Eliza, who had come out of the store to see them off, and also to see what was happening in the street.

"Gabe is a strange man. But he was always thought to be harmless," Amy said as they drove up the main street and turned off on the trail back to Broken Horseshoe Ranch.

"What is this goldmine he talks about?" Josh asked.

"Gabe reckons it's one that the Spanish mined, and they found a huge gold vein running along into a cave. The old man says he found a pile of gold nuggets there. His story is that the Spaniards left when they were run off by the local Indians. The Indian's Thunder God forbids taking any gold or silver out of the mountains, and they made sure that the Spaniards failed to leave with their spoils. But Gabe says he has a magic spell given to him by an old Indian, which means he can take the gold."

Josh was thinking about this tale. It all sounded extremely far-fetched. Then he realised Amy had slumped into silence as the buggy bumped its way along the trail. She was obviously shocked and tired after the shooting. He thought she would probably be in pain as well from the wound in her arm.

Josh drove on towards Broken Horseshoe Ranch. He, too, was silent. It had only been a short time since Amy had discovered him, covered in blood, which fortunately was not his, but he'd been unconscious and left alone in the desert. When he'd come to, uninjured apart from an enormous lump on his head, he'd lost his memory. The only thing on him, hidden in his boot, was a screwed up bit of paper. It said "Josh Barnes, go to Broken Horseshoe Ranch". Those written words went around and around in his brain. Had it been coincidence or fate? Josh had wondered, because the girl who'd found him, Amy Tanner, actually lived on that ranch.

"I've never seen Gabe whenever I've been out searching. He must go further around the Devil's Mountain," Amy blurted out.

"Is he still searching for a mine? Or has he found it?" Josh asked her.

"I don't know. From what we've just heard, he thinks he's found it and is trying to keep everybody else away from it."

"It's totally different from what I'm searching for. I'm looking for buried deposits of gold and silver coins and bars. That's hidden caches of Jesuit gold, not down mines. I hope we don't come across Gabe in our searches," Amy added with a shudder.

Was Amy's search any different from Gabe's? Josh wondered if searching for gold on the Devil's Mountain drove everyone mad. Would he and Amy end up like Gabe?

# CHAPTER THIRTY-TWO

The buggy travelled on over the barely perceptible trail. Amy gave a great sigh. Josh looked with concern at his companion. "Do you feel all right?" Amy was not looking good. He hoped this journey would end soon and he could place the girl in Leah's capable hands. The older woman, along with her husband, Ezra, had been living at Broken Horseshoe Ranch when Amy and her father Luke and brother Ben had arrived some months ago. Leah had plentiful herbal remedies, and her extensive practical knowledge was invaluable at moments like these.

"I'm feeling exhausted, that's all," was her reply. He knew that was an admission that Amy would not have liked to admit to. She must be feeling bad, he thought.

"It's shock after being shot, and loss of blood from the wound in your arm," said Josh. "Here, lean against me and rest your arm." He pulled Amy closer to him, supporting her.

Silence grew between them. But it was a companionable silence, and it gave Josh time to think. Amy was going out searching for this lost Jesuit gold, which was her father's dream, not hers. Luke, her father, had been weakened after a bout of flu that had killed his wife. On the doctor advising that the clear desert atmosphere would be good for his lungs, he had uprooted his son and daughter to follow his dream, searching for buried treasure. On their arrival, Luke had been too sick to undertake the search on his own and it had been left to Amy to hunt the elusive gold. Josh liked Luke but could never understand the man's determination to put his children in such a position only for the remote possibility of finding gold.

"How did I come to survive that gunshot?" Amy whispered.

Josh tilted his head to look down at her face, her words barely heard by him over the trundling noise made by the buggy. His eyes narrowed as he took in her puzzled expression. He felt she was thinking too much about the incident. Josh knew that dwelling on the situation that they had experienced, especially Amy, would not help either of them. But he thought it best to let her talk it out of her system.

"I should be dead! I was saved by a skillet of all things." Amy's words were now louder, but she had a break in her voice, as if quelling tears. Amy never cried. She was unused to tears. Josh knew that. After the death of her mother, Amy hadn't cried. She'd told him that one day, when she'd explained the family's arrival at Broken Horseshoe Ranch. Her father was ill, and she was needed to care for him and look after her younger brother. There was no time for her to mourn her mother.

Josh gave another quick look at Amy. Surely she wasn't going to cry? He couldn't cope with her crying; he couldn't cope with any woman crying. No way!

"Did you hear what that old man said to Manuel in the store?" Josh asked Amy, his hurried question hopeful of turning her thoughts from crying.

"No, I was talking to Eliza," was her reply. Her answer came after a big sniff. She swallowed hard, and the tears disappeared. Amy pushed back the two long braids she wore over her shoulders, wiped the back of her hand over her freckled nose, and gave another loud sniff. Her interest was now aroused by his question, and the tears had vanished, much to Josh's relief.

No memory of Josh's past life had returned since Amy

found him near death in the foothills of the Devil's Mountain. Relationships, especially with women, he had no recollections of, just vague drifting glimpses of elegantly dressed, beautiful ladies. But somehow, Josh knew that deep in his heart, not one of those beauties had ever touched him or made him feel the overwhelming tenderness that he felt for Amy. That wipe of her hand across her freckled snub nose and that final almighty sniff had caused Amy to grab his heart with her nail-bitten, calloused hands.

"What did he say?" Amy straightened up and stared at him inquiringly.

"They were wondering about the sheriff, and where he had gone. They said that he's gone missing, he's not been seen around for some days. Someone said they'd seen him riding out into the mountains, but no one has ever seen him come back." Josh exchanged a conspiratorial glance with Amy and they both smiled.

"I wonder where Sheriff Cody has disappeared to?" Amy said with a giggle.

"I wonder!" Josh replied. It had been good to hear her laugh, even if it was over the terrible business of Sheriff Cody that had occurred a few days ago. His disappearance was a secret everyone at Broken Horseshoe Ranch had to keep for their own safety and security.

"Eliza told me much more about the sheriff. The cash from his office has gone missing. Eliza said that they paid the sheriff money each month so that he could keep their store safe. He was asking them for protection money! Then, Eliza whispered to me she's heard that other money has gone missing from the bank."

"Whew! No one is sorry to see the back of that man.

Evil through and through he was, the town of Nowhere is a better place without him," Josh said.

They were nearing the ranch now, and the late afternoon sun was still hot. The Broken Horseshoe Ranch sign above the trail to the homestead shimmered in the heat of the sun and seemed never to get any nearer.

"I'll be glad to get back. Leah has a salve that will soothe this arm. It's stinging," said Amy.

The increasing pallor in Amy's face had worried Josh for some time, and he felt an overwhelming relief when he heard Ben shouting. "They're coming!"

"I love the way they always wave to us," Amy said, smiling at her brother who was waving his hat, and Ezra, the old man who'd always lived and looked after the ranch, waving his disreputable one. Chan waved both arms in the air in delight at their approach.

Josh turned to look at Amy and said in a loud voice, "We have got to stop doing this, Amy! It's no good, it's got to stop!"

# CHAPTER THIRTY-THREE

"Stop doing what?" Amy asked him, turning an astonished gaze towards him.

"One of us arriving home injured. First, you discovered me wounded and brought me back to the ranch. Then we found Chan with his dislocated arm and those horrible bruises and burns all over his body. And now you have to get in on the act!" Josh was delighted when he saw the bubble of laughter that erupted from Amy. She was still laughing when they drew up in front of the ranch house. Josh was perturbed by the overwhelming feeling of happiness that he had made Amy laugh. Surely, he shouldn't feel so deeply about this girl. It was something to be thought about later, on his own, at night.

Ben had rushed over to help with the horse and unload the buggy. However, when he saw the state his sister was in, he rushed to her side. "Your shirt is all covered in blood. Amy, what's happened to you?"

"Let's get everything inside, and then we'll tell you all about it. I've only got a scratch, a bullet grazed my arm, that's all. Don't look so worried, Ben, I'm fine," Amy said to her brother, giving him a pat on his shoulder as she climbed down from the buggy.

"Yet another bloodstained shirt!" Amy said to Josh as they unloaded the provisions. Through their joint laughter, Josh had horrible memories of his trudge through the searing heat of midday in a shirt caked with dried blood. He had been thankful it wasn't his blood – that went without saying. But it was a memory he wished he had forgotten.

"That wasn't my blood, Amy, unfortunately this blood

is yours," said Josh quietly, his face set hard with anger.

Their story was told. Amy's arm was re-dressed with Leah's home-made ointment, and the skillet was shown again and again. There was shock and horror at the terrible state that poor old Gabe had got into.

Luke especially shook his head in distress. "He shall be remembered in my prayers tonight. What a tragic way for a man to end his life in a confused state like that."

Sunset meant that the sun was dipping low in the sky. As night was drawing in, a complete darkness fell over the ranch. "It takes some getting used to, the great number of stars in the night sky. When we lived in the town, the lights from houses and occasional lamp somehow diluted the brightness of the stars," Luke said as he sat down on the porch.

The ramshackle porch that had been an unwary trap for the careless foot when Josh had arrived was no more. Widow Perkins, or Nancy, Mrs Tanner as she now was, had organised the men from the Dry Creek Ranch, her ranch, to make repairs. The porch had been the first item to have benefited. It now stretched out further than before, and had wide steps leading up to it, on three sides, and was no longer rickety or missing planks. She had even supplied a slat-backed rocking chair that was infinitely more comfortable for Luke, and he now preferred to sit out in the cool of the evening. Formerly, he had rushed off to his bed to rest. This porch was now more in use daily, and especially after supper.

"It's only been a few weeks since you married the Widow Perkins, Luke. What a difference she's made to this place!" Josh said.

Luke made a face, not quite a grimace, but verging on it. "That woman is like a whirlwind. She never stops moving and doesn't understand that not everyone can keep up with her," Luke said.

"But Pa, look at what she's done. We've got a proper porch now. No holes! And she's even getting another room built for us," Ben said.

"Yes, she's done a lot for us, Ben," said Amy. "Look around though, it's her animals that are grazing on our better land and she's going to cultivate the land with more vegetables that we can all eat and possibly sell for a profit."

"Miss Nancy said my garden will get bigger and Bill is going to help me all the time. The lady at the general store is going to buy from us. I can earn money for all of you!" The little Chinese boy, they reckoned about eleven years old, bounced on the bottom step in enthusiastic delight. "I can pay my way. That's how you say it, isn't that right, Josh?"

"Yes, Chan, that's the correct way to say it," said Josh, smiling down at the boy. He sat on the top step, long, muscled legs thrust out in front of him. His long, blonde hair was pushed back from his face with an impatient gesture. It was getting too long now, but he'd seen Ezra at work on Ben's hair and had backed away hurriedly from the scissors. Maybe one of Nancy's boys over at the Dry Creek Ranch was more expert at cutting hair. Ezra was not!

"I can't get over how different it all is now. I remember that day when Nancy arrived as the Widow Perkins and suggested you get married to her, Pa," Amy said. Her face had a reminiscent grin upon it.

"Remember, everyone, it was a marriage of convenience!" Luke made that clear to them all. Again! It was something that he constantly repeated. "Both ranches benefit. We have the year-round spring water, and she has the stock and the workforce. It was mutually beneficial."

"Yes, and remember, Sis, Nancy made us her step kids and we will inherit the Dry Creek Ranch. That means we inherit two ranches, Broken Horseshoe Ranch and Dry Creek Ranch." Ben's usual tactless way of speaking about whatever crossed his mind betrayed him yet again. "I mean that Pa and Nancy are..." His face showed his appalled confusion.

"It's okay, Ben, I know what you mean. I'm also delighted with that part of the arrangement. A sick man like me worries about leaving you both." Luke paused and looked very solemn, then he drank from his mug. It was filled with his everlasting coffee that he was never without. He always had a coffee in his hand. He put the mug down abruptly with a loud clatter onto the roughhewn table that had been placed on the porch beside his chair. "If I'd known what life was really like in this desert area at the foot of the Devil's Mountain, not only would I have never come, but I'd also have made certain that I never brought you two kids out here."

"But, Pa, you wanted to find the lost Jesuit gold. Remember, you've always wanted to search for it," Ben reminded him.

"That doctor told me desert air would make a new man of me. Far from it! I never thought we'd struggle to live and exist, and I'd have to watch my daughter ride out alone every day looking for the gold. Maybe it's a foolish thought to think that I should be able to find it when no one else could. But I was assured that the map was genuine, and all the circumstances surrounding it seemed to prove that. I actually felt that this would be the way out of all our problems." Luke stared off into the darkness, his face sunk into lines and hollows of illness and dejection.

Josh watched Amy's face. It clouded over at her father's words, and he felt he should say something to lift the depressing mood which had fallen on the group. "Well, Luke, she's not alone anymore. I'm here and I go with her now."

Luke drew in a breath before he spoke. "Yes, Josh, you go with her now. What happens when your memory returns? You may remember another life, another place, and people that you should be with. What happens then?"

# CHAPTER THIRTY-FOUR

Josh and Ben did the usual morning chores. It had become a routine, made easier now with Chan's arrival. The boy had learnt to cook whilst working at the cookhouse and had bacon, biscuits, and refried beans along with a hot pot of coffee ready for them all each morning. Ben went out to the stable to saddle Amy and Josh's horses, ready for their trip up the mountains. Josh shook out the bedding in the cool morning air before piling it up again in the corner of the room.

The sun showed only as a faint glow on the horizon, a red-gold promise of the morning sun. Nighttime could be cold or at least chilly after the heat of the day. The wooden shutters were opened and the morning air swept through the cabin. Standing on the porch, Josh gazed out at the wide-open space around him. It was an unfamiliar land to what he had known before. He knew that. But how did he know? And if he knew, why would nothing else enter this blank mind of his? The smell of the crispy bacon and the hot coffee tantalised him and, turning his back on the desert vista, he went into the cabin for his breakfast.

"How are you feeling this morning?" Josh asked Amy.

The girl had wandered out from her cupboard bedroom with its newspapered walls. The shadows under her eyes were dark, and she moved awkwardly. "I'm fine. My arm is stiff. I didn't sleep well, but once out and moving about, I'll be good."

Breakfast was eaten at the table in silence. It was too good to talk over. Luke didn't make an appearance. The older man was getting visibly weaker, and always had a coffee in his bedroom now each morning.

"What are your plans for today, boys?" Josh said, swallowing his last biscuit mouthful. Chan made the fluffiest biscuits he'd ever tasted.

"The garden needs weeding and watering as usual," Chan said, his eyes lighting up with pleasure.

Luke, on his arrival, had great ideas about gardening. He had determined to grow enough crops to make themselves self-sufficient, but he had been too inexperienced a gardener and too weak to cope with the work involved. It had been Chan who had taken over the garden. He loved it and made it prosper and grow and enjoyed every minute he worked in it.

"You like the garden, Chan," Amy smiled at the boy.

"Yes, Amy, I love doing it, and watching everything grow. Miss Nancy says she will take some of my stuff to sell at the general store. Then I can give Mr Luke real money for my keep!" The boy kept repeating this, as if to ensure that they would always have a place for him.

Amy rose from the table, carrying her plate to wash up. As she passed the boy, she stooped and gave him a hug. "That will be helpful if you earn money, Chan. But you do so much around the ranch, especially with the cooking. You earn your keep with us already."

The broad grin spreading over the Chinese boy's face made them all smile. He now had a healthy colour and was filling out. That emaciated look was almost gone, and his cuts and burns were healing. Josh thought Chan was so different now from the injured boy that Amy had bought from the cookhouse owner. They still knew little about the boy's past life. He seemed intent on keeping it secret. Josh thought he must've come over from China with an older member of his family. It didn't seem possible that he would have come alone on that long journey from China looking for work. But whilst his English was excellent in the everyday life they were living, it was impossible to conduct an in-depth conversation with the boy. Whether he didn't know enough English, or whether he wished to keep his secrets, it was hard to discover.

Ezra had joined them from the log cabin behind the ranch house, and he, Chan, and Ben waved Josh and Amy off on this new search. The night before, they had all pored over the maps and had decided on a fresh journey: going behind the marked cactus, and further up into the mountains. The ride during the early dawn was pleasant, the air still crisp and fresh. Movements amongst the rocks and scrubby vegetation showed the night critters scuttling back to hide from the dawning day's cruel sunshine.

"Does Gabe come along this trail?" Josh asked Amy.

"Sometimes. There is a branch off the trail when we come to the huge rocks. Ezra says Gabe turns off there and goes up and round the mountainside. There were old goldmines up there. Maybe that's where Gabe goes."

"You've never been tempted to go into the mines and look for silver or gold?" Josh asked as they rode along.

"No, thank you! Go into dark pits and caves. No, I'm too scared of rockfalls, snakes, and spiders, and other animals that can use them as lairs. I'll search above ground, thank you, perhaps digging down aways, but not into mines. There could even be black bears in them!" Amy said, throwing back her pigtails over her shoulders. Her snub nose wrinkled at the very thought of the dark, dreary mines.

Josh smiled at the girl, loving the way her freckles danced when she screwed her face up in disgust. "I thought you weren't afraid of anything!" Josh teased her.

"Ezra says it's only a fool that isn't scared of anything. I can give you a list of what I'm scared of if you like!" Amy retorted. "And some of those mines have booby-traps."

"Booby-traps? Who set them and why...?" Josh began, when Amy interrupted him.

"Look at those clouds up ahead. Is that lightning in them?" Amy interrupted Josh, her voice now harsh with alarm.

"Yes, that will be good. We'll get some rain," Josh said. He wondered why Amy had stopped and was staring fixedly at the black clouds approaching.

"Yes. It is lightning, and I can hear thunder in the distance!" Amy's voice was filled with dread and her face was white with fear.

# CHAPTER THIRTY-FIVE

"A storm! It's not just rain, it's going to be a severe storm. We must seek shelter. We must get out of the floor of this canyon. It's a deathtrap down here! Up there! See the track going up past those enormous boulders? There's a small ledge with an overhanging rock. It might even be a cave. As fast as we dare, we must get up there, Josh." Amy's voice was harsh and shrill, with the urgent need for action.

Josh didn't argue. One look at the expression on Amy's face told him to do exactly as she said, and as speedily as he could. Each horse was urged to pick its way around rocks and boulders, between cacti and scrubby vegetation, all the while heading for higher ground. Upwards they went. It was slow going, but the urgency Amy felt had communicated itself to Josh and, he felt, even to the horses. Or was it the approaching storm? Every moment it seemed to Josh that Amy looked at those approaching storm clouds with increasing concern. Was it fanciful or did even the horses glance back at those clouds that loomed ever closer?

Guiding his horse up the rocky cliff path after Amy, Josh could see the lightning flashes clearer now. The occasional rumble of thunder was becoming louder as it got closer to them. The difficult pathway became narrower and steeper. Still, Amy urged her horse upwards.

Amy dismounted and looked back at Josh. "We'll get off our horses now, Josh, and lead them. It's tricky going round these boulders, but it's the last part of the climb before we reach the ledge." It took some gentle coaxing, but the horses gallantly made that last part and they all arrived safely on the ledge.

Drawing a deep breath, Josh took off his hat, wiping the sweat that was running down his face with the back of his hand. The air was thick and heavy with the approaching storm clouds. The canyons always seemed quiet when they travelled through them, but there was now an eerie stillness that had fallen over the land. Where they stood, the canyon stretched around to the right of them and then extended to the left further up the mountain. It ended abruptly in a sheer rocky cliff face.

"This is quite a big ledge. There's plenty of room up here. I wouldn't have thought it so big when we looked up from the canyon floor. Is that a cave behind us?" Amy said and pointed to the dark hole in the centre of the ledge. Josh smiled to himself as Amy stood back, waiting for him to have a look at it. He remembered her dislike of dark spaces and the insects and snakes that inhabited them. Josh shrugged and walked towards it, peering inside it whilst standing back a safe distance.

"Is there anything in it?" Amy asked, following behind him. She stood well back. Amy was leaving it to Josh to check out the cave!

"I don't know. I don't think it goes very far back, but it's dark in there."

Amy looked at the approaching storm clouds, which were almost upon them, and the more frequent flashes of lightning, and then the cave opening. "I think we should see if we can shelter in there." She picked up a rock and threw it into the cave. It only reached the entrance.

"That might work. I'll go nearer and have a go. And try to flush out any critters!" Josh said with a laughing glance back at Amy. He threw a few more rocks, and with a scrubby branch, he went to the entrance and brushed it clear. "It's not a real deep cave, Amy, it's just the overhang, and it's empty of wildlife. I swept it clean to make certain. No snakes, no spiders, and definitely no bears or lions."

Amy stuck her tongue out at him. The childlike gesture, so unusual from the normally solemn Amy, took Josh aback and then he laughed. Smiling back at him, Amy brought the horses under the overhang and tethered them to a branch of a tree that was clinging on to the rock face. She took her water bottle and turned to Josh. "Take a drink now, keep your bottle with you, and grab your blanket. Wrap it around you and we'll hunker down in the entrance to the cave until the storm passes."

Josh took his water bottle and his blanket and joined her in the cave, out of the path of the oncoming storm. "Why did you climb up so high?"

"Ezra and I got caught in a storm like this one, and this is what he showed me to do. It's the only sure way to survive a storm in the warmer months. If the Thunder God roars, take cover! Ezra said if the horses freak out and race away, we've got our water bottles and blankets, we should survive."

Josh sipped his water. Only one sip. Since his arrival at Broken Horseshoe Ranch, and his journeys with Amy out into the foothills and deserts surrounding the Devil's Mountain, he had learnt how important water was for survival. Leaning back against the rock, he watched the massive black clouds form into an anvil shape coming closer to them. They filled the sky and loomed threateningly over them.

"It's going to be a big one. There looks to be a lot of rain in those clouds," Amy said.

The wind grew stronger and Josh edged closer to Amy

and pulled her further into the cave, putting his blanket around her shoulders. Sudden gusts of a ferocious strength attacked them as if determined to throw them onto the canyon floor far beneath them. Lightning flashed again and again, the brilliance of its flashes made their eyes ache and the whole canyon lit up as if the moon had escaped to land within it. The thunder rumbled and then crashed, its noise reverberating from rock face to rock face, and up and down the canyon walls until they felt as if they were being bombarded with gunfire.

"Never have I been in a storm like this! This lightning is unbelievable and the noise from that thunder is deafening," Josh shouted at Amy, his words being blown away from him into the storm.

"Wait for the rain!" Amy whispered into his ear.

Amy nestled into his body. Josh, realising that she was grateful for his warmth and the security he gave her, took pleasure in the fact that she was beginning to trust him. Amy felt right in his arms. He was certain, despite his blank memory, that he'd never cared for a woman as he did for Amy. If only he knew who he was! Josh felt that a man with no name and no past could not in all conscience court a girl like Amy. Despite the increasing violence of the storm around him, Josh was sure every moment spent close to this girl would be treasured by him in the days to come.

The ground trembled as the lightning and thunder echoed round and round. The horses moved restlessly, made increasingly anxious by the clamour of the storm. Josh crept forward on his hands and knees to secure the horses to yet another branch.

"I don't dare stand up. I could be blown off this ledge," he shouted at Amy. "I've made the horses more secure. Will they be all right?"

Cupping her hands around her mouth and coming closer to his ear, Amy shouted at him. "These horses are used to the summer storms. They dislike them, but I'm sure they'll stay up here with us. They know they are safer here than down on the open ground."

The rain fell and burst into a tumbling torrent from the sky. Josh was horrified. The rain seemed to fall every which way, in wild, windy spurts slashing into their faces and sweeping across the ledge. "I've never known rain like this," he shouted to Amy. "Thank goodness you spotted this ledge."

The increase in the wind and rain sweeping along the rock ledge so far above the canyon threatened to force them off. Each gust became wilder and stronger, tearing at their clothes and the blankets wrapped around them. With so little to cling on to, they could only huddle together and hope!

# CHAPTER THIRTY-SIX

As suddenly as it had come, the storm was over. The dark clouds moved over the mountains, and the wind lessened before dying away completely. Sun blazed down on them as the last of the clouds vanished over the horizon. The air seemed to sizzle, and the earth lost its dank, wet look from the heavy rain and returned to its usual dusty desert.

Josh stood up and shook out the blanket. Drops of water flew off from it, almost hissing into steam as they landed on the rapidly heating earth. He looked back at Amy, who still sat on her blanket. Their closeness under those blankets would always be a special moment for him. Why that should be, Josh couldn't fathom, but it worried him. A man in his position had no business having feelings for this girl, or any girl. He knew he'd never act on them, and he'd make sure that Amy never knew of his real feelings for her. Still, it worried him.

"There's no hurry, Josh," Amy said. Sitting on the ledge, she removed the blanket from her shoulders and shook it out.

"Shouldn't we continue our search?"

"Not yet, we wait for at least an hour," was her reply.

Josh stood on the edge of the ledge, looking down at the canyon below. But at that remark, he turned to Amy. "Why wait?"

"That was a very heavy downpour of rain. This is a narrow canyon with steep sidewalls, but if you look closely at those walls, you can see high watermarks made by the passage of previous floods. After rains like we've had today, it's likely that we will get flash floods coming through here. That's why we wait, to make sure there's no chance of one. Ezra made me promise to always wait for a spell after heavy rain."

"Flash floods? That's unbelievable, it's so dry down in the canyon. I can't imagine... But I know it's best to do what Ezra says. He knows this country and its weather." Words failed Josh as he stared down at the canyon floor below him and the narrow, rocky walls climbing up each side. Shrugging, he came back and joined Amy after checking the horses. Josh was surprised at how well they had stood calmly throughout the storm. "You were right, Amy, they are used to these storms. I thought they'd be scared."

Patting both horses, Josh murmured to them, praising them. Wanting to stretch his legs because he felt restless at this enforced stay on the ledge, he walked further along it to the end of the rock face. There was a gap in the cliff face, a small crevice. No one could have seen it from below, and he wouldn't have seen it if he hadn't walked along the ledge.

"There is a small cave along here. I'm going up to the entrance," he called to Amy. As he walked further into it, he was aware of Amy rising to her feet and following him.

Sunlight, previously obscured by the last clouds of the storm, suddenly shone its full force into the crevice.

"Oh, my! Oh good grief!" Josh pointed to the carving brought out clearly by the sun's rays. Its carved features were shown in sharp relief with the shadows highlighting the symbols carved in the rock. Illuminated by the sun, it had caught his attention.

"It's a cross!" Amy breathed into Josh's ear as she came up behind him to peer over his shoulder at what he had discovered. "You found a cross, Josh. I'm certain that it's a Jesuit cross! It's exactly what we were looking for."

Both of them moved closer to the carved symbol and became silent at their astonishing discovery.

"It's a cross, but what are the markings below it?" Josh asked, tracing it with his finger. A superb carver had first incised the Jesuit cross, but below the cross there was another symbol, carved with the same skill. "It's a circle, with an arrow in it and... look, Amy." Josh was still fingering the symbol of the cross, and then he dropped his finger to trace the circle and the number beneath it beside the arrow. "The number is a twelve. What does it mean?" he added.

"It's pointing further along the canyon, and surely it must mean measurement?" Amy said. "But what measurement?" She had come up to join Josh, and she, too, traced the cross symbol with a forefinger.

"What a find, Amy! It shows that we are on the right path." Josh felt his smile widen and Amy grinned back at him. He continued speaking, "I was uncertain about..." Josh stopped speaking, too embarrassed to continue.

"You mean you didn't believe my father's crazy ideas about Jesuit treasure?" Amy teased him, laughing at the guilty expression on his face. "Come on, admit it! You didn't believe a word of it!"

"Well, no, not really," Josh replied, embarrassed at Amy's teasing and at how correct she had been. Then Josh looked at the girl. "Well, what about you? Did you believe wholeheartedly in the treasure story?"

Amy's face took on a rosy tinge. She tried to think of an answer to his question. Before she could plan one, they both turned in alarm. There was an incredible noise coming down the canyon towards them. It was a roar, not unlike the thunder of the past hour, but far louder, and it was getting noisier and nearer. This incredible noise was accompanied by a grating, crashing, banging sound that blasted its way towards them into the canyon.

Josh stared, wide-eyed and white-faced, as the noise got closer. "What is it? Will it reach up to us?"

# CHAPTER THIRTY-SEVEN

The great roaring noise came ever nearer. The sound was as loud as the previously noisy thunder had been. Accompanying it was a grinding, crashing noise that made Amy want to cover her ears. She stood staring anxiously down the canyon.

"Amy! My goodness! You were so right. We would have been... I don't know what to say..." Josh gazed open-mouthed at the wall of water that had rounded the far corner of the canyon. Tumbling spume and sprays of murky water rushed down the canyon towards them. Several feet below them, the wall of water bounced and crashed off the cliff faces, rock ledges, and boulders. Spray from the crashing waves on the canyon walls erupted high in the air.

"The water is full of debris! There's a giant tree trunk there. Rocks and boulders are being thrown along in that enormous wave of water," shouted Josh over the horrific noise.

Amy wasn't attending to his astonished cries. When he turned towards her, he saw she was talking to and soothing the horses.

"What's wrong with them?" Josh rushed over to her side and also began calming the large, grey mare that they used mostly for ranch work. A solid, dependable horse, if getting on in years, her eyes were rolling, and she obviously disliked the roaring water rushing along the canyon floor beneath her.

"Hush, Bella!" Amy's soothing tones to her favourite horse seemed to quieten both animals. "They've never seen or heard anything like this before. It's no wonder they're frightened."

Silence! The water had gone as suddenly as it had arrived. The stillness that descended upon the mountains and the canyon beneath them was unbelievable. Both horses relaxed and stood quietly, their anxious panting breaths stilled. Amy sank down upon her blanket and wiped her face with the back of a hand.

Josh looked down at her with an even greater respect than he'd felt for her before. "You saved our lives, Amy. If you hadn't acted on the knowledge Ezra gave to you, we'd have been in amongst that lot!" His gesture encompassed the desolate scene below them. "What happens now? Do the Four horsemen of the Apocalypse ride through next?" Josh joked.

"Don't tempt fate!" Amy said and rose gracefully to her feet. Then she pointed across the canyon. "Look at those boulders! They were tossed from one side of the canyon to the other. Ugh! I've often heard that flash floods are frightening things, and that they claimed many lives. I never believed that they could be so powerful. I do now!"

She began leading the horses down the treacherous path, then she stopped and looked back at Josh. "And now the desert blooms! The rain makes the desert come to life and we get a wonderful display of flowers. There will be flowers everywhere, and the desert becomes the most wonderful sight you've ever seen."

They led the horses down the winding, precipitous path that they had ridden up only a short time earlier. Neither of them spoke of returning to the ranch. Unspoken consent between them made them follow the Jesuit carved symbols. They turned, following the direction of the arrow.

"I wonder what the unit of measurement was for the

Jesuits," Amy said thoughtfully.

"I should think it's paces, surely. That's what everyone has with them, their feet. It's a basic universal measurement. So now that we are down below the carved symbol, we just pace out the required number," Josh said, standing still and looking up at the entrance of the cave and then further along to the hidden crevice with its secret carving. He walked along the canyon floor until he was directly beneath the symbol.

Pools of water lay, evaporating in the sun's glare. They stumbled around the boulders that had been hurled any which way. Small trees and scrubby tangles of vegetation had obviously been uprooted and thrown around in the water. It was difficult pacing because there was so much stuff in their way. It was Josh who did the pacing. They had both reasoned that the Jesuits would be male and that a masculine stride would be essential.

As they went round the canyon, they were faced by a soaring blank wall of rock.

"It's a dead end. That's a blank wall of rock in front of us. Where to now?" Josh said.

"Oh Josh, you are right and it is a dead end. Why would that carving lead us towards a blank cliff face?"

Josh walked over to stand beneath the rock face. He looked up at the soaring slab of the mountain in front of him. "Amy! I found another symbol! Up there!" Josh clambered over the tumbled mess of rocks and vegetation left behind after the water's surge. Here, at the end of the canyon, the rainstorm must have produced a maelstrom of waters. "I think there's been a whirlpool here. Everything has been tumbled around but if we can climb over these rocks, the number I can see carved in the cliff face will be easier to look at."

"You must have keen eyes, Josh! It's good that you spotted both carvings. I'm glad that I found you in the desert, after all. You have a better eye than I have. I'd never have seen them. I'm coming over to climb up beside you and get a better look."

Josh led the way, pushing aside some of the vegetation. "Take care, Amy, it's slippery and..." His voice abruptly ceased, his foot stopped in midair, and his whole body froze as still as a statue as he stared at the ground in front of him. Then Josh put out his hand to stop Amy from going any further. "Amy, get back to the horses now. There's no need for you to see this. Go, Amy!"

# CHAPTER THIRTY-EIGHT

Amy did not move away. Instead of obeying Josh's shouted instructions, she moved forward and peered over his shoulder. Her gasp of horror alerted Josh to her presence by his side.

"Oh, no! What's happened? Do you think the storm caused this?" Her voice was only a whisper, but it seemed loud to him.

Josh watched Amy as she stood her ground beside him. He knew she was used to Western life and its hardships, the common everyday injuries, and the sad and sometimes appalling incidents and deaths that had hardened her to some extent. But not to this! Josh knew he had been right after all. She should not have looked. But her face showed her determination to stand firmly on the ground, as firmly as her tiny, square-toed boots would let her. Amy took in a deep breath.

"Where is his head?" Amy's whispered words echoed around the canyon walls and seemed to whisper back at them. "I can't see his head. Josh, where is his head?"

"I don't know. I think we'd better look for it." Josh answered Amy, but not in his usual voice. His words were stilted and forced. "Do you know him?"

The man lay like a child's tattered rag doll. His arms were flung out wide, one leg straight out, the other one bent awkwardly beneath him. Clad in worn canvas trousers, his braces holding them up were over a plaid shirt. The worn, scuffed boots and his clothes were typical of many of the old-timers, and of any gold prospector in the mountains. The long, thin gash of blood at his neck was the only sign of injury. But it was enough! That was where his head had been cut off!

Some time later, Josh yelled to Amy, who was searching further along on the opposite side of the canyon to him. "I don't think it's anywhere here. What do we do now, Amy? Do we leave him or take his body back to Nowhere?"

Amy clambered back towards Josh and the body. She was panting hard by the time she reached him. "It's getting hotter in this canyon, and after the rain, it's sticky and oppressive. We need to get out of this heat," she said to Josh as she joined him, looking down at the man's body.

Neither of them had relished their search for the unknown man's head. But both felt that it was the correct and Christian thing to do. If it hadn't been such a terrible moment and a gruesome search, Josh would have smiled at Amy's face as she clambered over rocks and peered under the brush that lay everywhere. Her little nose was screwed up, and her mouth was tight and her lips pressed together to hold back the emotions that he knew she was feeling. He felt them as well as Amy. How could any other human being do this evil deed?

"What shall we do?" Josh repeated. He didn't know the Western way, not only of life but of death. A stranger here, he felt Amy should decide. When she found him unconscious, with no possessions, she'd also found another man dead with gunshot wounds. They'd left him where he lay. Neither had felt any guilt at leaving him. They hadn't the means to get him back to civilisation. It had been necessary for their survival. But this man? "Amy, what do you say we should do?" Josh said, staring at the girl.

Amy had screwed up her nose, yet again, and put her head to one side while she thought the problem through.

First, she looked at the man, then Josh saw her gaze slide up to the carved symbol they'd spent so much time looking for.

"I think we should take him back to Nowhere. I think he's been a decent chap by the look of him, possibly an old prospector. He's neat and tidy. At least that's what we can see of him." Josh nodded in agreement with this. "A man shot in these hills is no unusual occurrence sadly, but this..." Amy couldn't begin to say it, and only gestured towards the body.

"And?" Josh enquired.

"The carving! If we tell where we found him, others may come to look for the head and see that symbol and..."

"And carry on our search," interrupted Josh. "I agree we take his body back to Nowhere, Amy, I think we have to. But do we need to tell where we found him?"

"No, I don't think we need to tell exactly where we found him. His clothes are wet. He could have been killed anywhere along the path of the flash flood. I doubt he would have been killed here, caught up in the flood, and remained in the same spot. Do you?" Amy said.

Josh thought for a moment, looked round at the debris-strewn canyon and slowly shook his head. "No, Amy, I think you are in the right of it. There's no telling where he was killed. It could have been much further down the canyon. In fact, I think it was a useless task searching for his head. It could be anywhere along the path of the flood. There is no need to pinpoint this location when we take him back to Nowhere."

Josh stared up at the symbol carved above him. His muscular shoulders tapered down to the lean hips and the long legs. His head was thrust back, the overlong hair spilling over his shirt collar. Josh ran a hand through his long, blonde hair in desperation at the predicament in which they found themselves. He was at a loss. He knew he had been a person who could make decisions. But after the blow on his head and the blank memory he now had, decision-making seem to be difficult, if not impossible. "After all our hard work searching for this, I'd hate for someone else to come in and find our clues to the Jesuit gold." He walked over to the body of the old man and looked down at it. "Now all we have to do is get this poor fellow back to Nowhere."

The distaste he felt for the task was overwhelming, and as he looked at Amy, he saw her already ashen face lose its last vestiges of colour at the thought of the urgent task they had in front of them.

Josh looked at the pathetic body in dismay and confessed. "But I don't know how we will manage it. How do we get the poor man back to Nowhere? How will we do it? He has no horse with him. How can we get him back to Nowhere?"

# CHAPTER THIRTY-NINE

Josh watched as the practical side of Amy fought off her distaste at the task that presented itself to them. How he admired that plucky side of her character.

"Bella is the quietest and easiest to give strange tasks to. If we get him slung over her, we can both ride on Star. He's stronger than Bella and he'll carry our combined weight easily. But the man's neck?" Amy looked at Josh. She had got so far in her plans, but looking at the gaping hole left on the body when the man had been decapitated, Josh could see, had her at a loss.

"You sort out the horses, give me a blanket and I'll sort out the man's body," Josh said. Horrendous as the task was, he felt he should do it on his own, and spare Amy.

A short time later and they were ready to travel to Nowhere. The man, securely bound and covered with a blanket, lay across Bella. The horse had rolled her eyes and stamped her feet uneasily when she looked round at her burden, but she had accepted it.

Amy stood beside the man's body. She bowed her head and said a prayer for him. "It's the least I can do," she said and prepared to mount Star with Josh.

As one, they both stood for a moment, staring up at the carved symbol above them. Amy sighed, "If only we could have got up there to have a look!"

"It's not going away," said Josh as they rode off. "We can come back from Nowhere and continue the search. Now we have a clue we know exactly where to begin our search."

The journey was tedious and distressing, knowing the burden that Bella was carrying behind them. They rode on, taking only a brief break to stretch their legs and drink. As they stood beside Star, Josh turned to Amy. "Where do we go? Who will take the man? After all, Sheriff Cody is missing?"

"I wonder where Cody has gone to?" Amy gave a conspiratorial smile to Josh, which he returned with a laugh.

"I wonder? But we both know where he's gone, and that's a secret we must keep. Knowing what happened to him could place us all in danger. It's a dangerous secret everyone at Broken Horseshoe Ranch has to keep. "

"True, but we will have to remember to look worried and concerned about poor missing Sheriff Cody," Amy said.

"Someone else will be in charge by now. They may even have a new sheriff in place. Best thing is to take him to the general store and Manuel will know what to do," said Josh.

They stood for a while in the shade of the rocks, neither of them wishing to travel on. But eventually they put the water bottles away and prepared to mount Star. Josh, his hand on the saddle, thought for a moment and then turned to Amy. "What were we doing out there?"

Amy stared at him in surprise. "Oh! I'd never thought of that. You're right, Josh. We must have a story for everybody. We must be able to say what we were doing and where we found him. I think we should say we found him over by the trail leading to the Mesa. That's well away from our Jesuit Trail. But why were we out there?"

Amy's puzzlement amused Josh. She bit her lip, screwed up her nose as always, and tilted her head on one side, just like a bird. It was a small bird she reminded him of, but his memory failed him yet again. He couldn't remember what bird! The journey, holding Amy in front of him on the one horse, had been no hardship for Josh. Every moment he held her in the shelter of his arms would be treasured by him. Hiding his feelings from her had become of great importance to him, but now he had these precious moments to treasure in the dark nights.

"I know! I've arrived at my uncle's ranch to see the wild West, meet my estranged family members, and..." Here, Josh paused for dramatic effect. "... And I have a treasure map to the lost Spanish silver mines!"

"Well done!" Amy applauded him. "That should go down well. There are so many gold and silver maps floating about, you will just have another one. Knowing the area, I was guiding you. Yes, that's a place we found him sorted, and the reason for being out there." Amy glanced with distaste at the body slung over Bella. "Let's get him to town and prepared for a decent Christian burial."

On their entry into the Main Street of Nowhere, they were met by horrified onlookers. Their progress towards the general store was hindered by the many questions and gasps of horror by the folk that came to gawp at the body slung over the horse.

When Manuel walked out of his store and stood watching their arrival, Josh called out to him. "Is Sheriff Cody back yet?"

"No, he's still missing. But the Preacher is the man in charge of Nowhere at the moment. Hey, you boy! Go fetch the Preacher!" Manuel replied.

Amy and Josh dismounted, Josh tying the horses to the hitching rail.

"Who is he? Where did you find him?" The questions came at Josh and Amy from all sides. But the most frequent and difficult one for them to answer was, "where's his head?"

"We couldn't find his head," Amy whispered.

A voice, high-pitched and hysterical, cried out from the back of the crowd. "It's the Devil! He's stalking the mountains again! It's the curse of the Devil's Mountain. The Devil has returned!"

# CHAPTER FORTY

The voices went silent. "The curse" was murmured through the crowd, in whispers at first, and then with an increasing clamour.

"Sheriff Cody around?" Amy asked Manuel.

"No, he's still not back and now there's talk of missing money," Eliza said, coming up to Amy. "Remember, I told you before?" At Amy's murmured "yes", Eliza continued speaking. "Other shops and businesses were also paying him protection money. Cody was getting money from so many people."

"Oh, no!" Amy exclaimed. "Then who's the sheriff now? We need to take this poor man's body to him."

A dark figure could be seen walking purposefully towards them. He wore black trousers, with a flowing black coat swirling around him with the sudden gust of wind that blew down the main street. Dust swirled in tiny eddies, spinning wildly before collapsing into a sighing heap.

Josh wiped his brow again with the back of his hand. He'd lost count of the number of times he'd done that this day. The heat was still heavy after the storm. It hadn't cleared the air at all. They'd made good time to Nowhere, Josh realised, surprised at the speed of their journey.

The noisy crowd of people around him was unsettling. A prickling sensation at the back of his neck caused his hairs to rise, and he knew that someone was watching him. Not the usual interest aroused by a stranger. No, this was a malevolence that he had aroused in someone. Josh felt certain that this unknown person wished him harm. Trying to appear casual, Josh looked around the crowd, still talking and pointing at the headless body. Nothing. Not one person seemed intent on him. But still, that feeling persisted.

"Preacher! What's going to happen now?" Manuel pushed forward to the front of the crowd to speak to the approaching preacher. "Preacher, there's no sheriff. You're the nearest we've got to a person of authority. So what should we do with this poor headless guy?"

"How about the Preacher for the sheriff? I reckon he'd be a good one!" The cry went up from the back of the crowd. It was taken up by others who shouted. "Preacher for sheriff!"

Josh looked around at the faces. From being angry and sad at the arrival of the dead body, the faces were now eager and excited.

Manuel raised a hand for the crowd to be silent. "Most of you folks know the sheriff is missing and we don't know when he's going to return. How about we ask the Preacher to stand in for Cody?"

Eager yells of agreement rose into the dusty air. "How about it, Preacher? Will you act as sheriff for now until we get a replacement for Cody?" Manuel said, with a few cheers following his remark.

In the meantime, the Preacher had joined Josh and was staring at the body. "If no one else..." he began.

Manuel slapped him on the back before the Preacher could finish. "That's fine and dandy. Folks, we have a new sheriff!"

Cheers greeted this. The Preacher caught Josh's eye. "I'm a fool to take this on, but someone has to keep this lot in line." Josh gave a sympathetic smile to the Preacher who was shaking his head at how he had been easily manoeuvred by Manuel into taking on the position of sheriff.

Amy had been ushered into the general store by Eliza for coffee and sympathy. She had cast an enquiring glance at Josh before she followed the older woman, but at his nod, she continued into the general store.

As she passed him by, he whispered to her. "You go in with Eliza. I'll finish up with the Preacher," and he followed the man in black to the sheriff's office.

To Josh's surprise, the Preacher took charge and dealt efficiently with the situation. "You two take their horses to the livery stable. Untie the body and place him in the back of the sheriff's office. I'll be there shortly."

As Josh stood back and let the Preacher take charge, sudden exhaustion swept over him, and he felt his legs beginning to buckle. The Preacher must have realised how tired Josh was because he grabbed his arm. "You need coffee. I have a pot ready brewed. It's not every day that you find a headless corpse!" After a coffee with the Preacher, Josh explained where they had found the man and what they had been doing. The plan of action outlined by Amy and himself before their return to Nowhere had proved invaluable. The Preacher had been satisfied by all of it. Thankfully, Josh left the Preacher and made for the general store.

Following Manuel into the general store, Josh stopped in the doorway at the overwhelming coolness that swept over him. The smells of the general store surrounded him. There were dry goods, oil for lamps, cooking shovels and tools for minors and prospectors, and everyday food staples that everyone needed.

"You look as if you need a coffee, Josh," Eliza said. He agreed. The one he'd had already from the Preacher had done little to quench his thirst. Eliza poured him out a cup and he drank it all down in one thirsty go. "Another one?"

Josh was still thirsty! "Yes please, and thank you, Eliza, and you, Manuel. I needed that." Josh smiled at the woman. Her round moon face broke into the most charming smile and she patted his arm. "You surely did," she laughed.

Amy walked over to Josh with a few parcels in her arms. "While I'm here, I'll get a few essentials. We can carry some back now the horses have rested," Amy said.

"Good idea. I'll go down and get the horses from the livery stables and bring them back here," said Josh.

"Bella will be glad to be relieved of her burden. There's nothing else we need to do for the body, is there?" Amy asked both Manuel and Eliza.

"Nothing, child, you've done plenty bringing him in for burial," said Eliza. "Get those horses, Josh. They'll have been fed and rested, and it's best you get home before dark. Especially now there's a killer on the loose."

Josh thanked Eliza and began walking down Main Street. There had been another false-fronted shop built in town since they'd last been to Nowhere. There was nothing to show what it was going to be, so Josh paused, hoping to get a glimpse. He was conscious of a fast moving horse riding up the street. As he was intent on the new shop, he was unaware that the horse had picked up speed and the rider, wearing a scarf pulled up over his lower face and a hat pulled low, was riding straight for him.

Manuel's voice rang out down Main Street. "Josh! Look out, Josh!"

# CHAPTER FORTY-ONE

Manuel's shout made Josh jump and whirl around to see the oncoming horse. Josh's eyes widened in horror. That cry from Manuel had alerted him to his danger. His reaction was fast and immediate. He could see the large horse was pounding towards him at full gallop. In the seconds it took to realise his danger, the horse was almost upon him. The flaring nostrils, the enlarged eyes were accompanied by the drumming of its hooves as it hurtled towards him along the dirt-packed road.

A superhuman strength seemed to take over Josh's body. With no conscious thought on his part, he flung himself to one side. He landed face first in the dirt and dust. But as the horse's hooves passed him by, Josh raised himself on his elbows to look at the horse and rider who had been intent on mowing him down. As the dust cleared from his fall, he saw black, shiny, leather boots embossed with silver patterns on them. His eyes followed the horse as it rode past him.

As he did so, the figure on the horse half turned back towards him and shouted at him. "Next time! I'll get you next time!"

Raising himself still further, and struggling to get up, Josh stared after the masked rider. Hunched over the horse, the man was swallowed up in a cloud of dust which swirled behind him and he was soon out of view.

Manuel, who had shouted, and with that cry had saved Josh's life, ran up to him. Eliza and Amy ran out of the store after hearing the shouts from Manuel. Passers-by on the street also gravitated to Josh, shouting and talking about this strange new occurrence. Shakily, Josh rose to his feet, brushing the dust off his clothes with his hat. He was unhurt but shaking slightly after his near-death experience.

"You were nearly a goner! That man was riding straight for you." Manuel held out his hand to steady Josh as he got to his feet.

"Thanks to you, Manuel, he didn't kill me. I would have been a goner if you hadn't shouted at me," Josh said, holding out his hand to shake that of his rescuer.

"What happened, Josh?" Amy's concern was mirrored on her face, and Josh couldn't help hoping it was more than she would have felt for just any acquaintance.

Explanations over, Josh was ushered back to the general store and given yet more coffee.

"Did you know him, Josh?" Manuel asked. "It surely looked deliberate to me. That man was going to run you down, and only you. He rode past a few others out on the street and then set his eyes upon you. He got the horse going real fast and then rode it straight at you. What have you done, Josh, to get someone so riled up at you?" The question was kindly meant, but both Josh and Amy tensed, and a glance was exchanged between them.

It was Amy who replied, "Josh knows no one here. Must've been someone out to attack anyone. Could have been any person just walking along the street," Amy said.

Manuel stared from Josh to Amy, and back again. "If you say so," he said. But his eyes held a growing suspicion, although he remained silent.

"I know of no one who would want to kill me. Amy is correct. Must've been someone pulling a stupid stunt," Josh said.

"Josh, do you need anything bathed or...?" began Eliza, fussing around Josh, worried by everything that had happened and, as always, eager to help.

"No, I thank you, Eliza," Josh said. "Thank you, both of you, Manuel. You have been a real lifesaver! Thanks again." Josh put his hand out to the other man, who shook it warmly.

The Mexican pulled his trousers up over his ample girth, and then shook Amy by the hand, a broad smile on his swarthy face.

Eliza, eager not to be outdone, threw her arms around Amy and clasped her to her ample bosom. "Take care, little one. I hear you have a stepmother now. Mrs Nancy is loud and bossy, but she has a heart of gold. Let her help you. You've taken care of your brother and the sick Papa long enough!"

Amy hugged Eliza back, and Josh could see that she was close to tears at the warmth of the chubby Mexican woman towards her.

"Come now, you're to go down to the Preacher, and then for your horses. We will watch over you both," Manuel said, and ushered them out of the doorway. He took a position on the boardwalk with his arms folded, but in a position of readiness and alert.

Without another word, Amy and Josh left the store and, with their Mexican Guardian Angels hovering in front of the general store, they walked the short distance to the sheriff's office. The wooden building was so new, they were almost overpowered by the smell of freshly cut timber. A significant glance was exchanged between them as Josh pushed open the door.

"Sheriff Preacher," said Amy. She was uncertain of what she should call the man now that he'd taken on this new role.

"Call me 'Preacher'! Only being a sheriff until they find a genuine mug who will take this darn job!" He half rose from his chair and gestured them to sit on the two hard chairs in front of a wooden table. Another door behind him was firmly shut. Josh presumed that the headless body lay within that room. A tall cupboard was against the wall with posters pinned up alongside it. They were wanted posters, each one having a price beneath the picture or drawing of a wanted man. Josh tried to look at the pictures without the man realising what he was doing. Amy's sly smile at him made him know she had guessed he was searching for his own face!

Josh spoke first. "We are about to head back to the ranch. Do you need anything further from us concerning the dead man?"

The Preacher scratched his nose, his prominent nose, nodded his head a few times and then spoke. "No, he's been identified as an old prospector called Bert. No other name, just 'Bert'. He was looking for a silver mine. Last time he was in the saloon, he reckoned he was on the trail. Maybe he found it, and that's what got him killed."

Again, he scratched his nose and shifted uncomfortably in his chair. "No sense looking for his head. Some critter will have taken it by now. We'll bury him, say a few prayers over him, and that's Bert." The Preacher stood up, a lengthy process as he had to unfold his long legs. "Unfortunate for you. Best get the girl back to the ranch. A terrible shock for a lass like her. You've got the new Mrs Tanner looking out for you now. Quite a lady, your new stepmother! I'll be watching to see how all that works out!" The Preacher shook their hands and opened the door for them, showing them his true southern ways. "Ha ha, quite a lady was the Widow Perkins! And now she's a Mrs Tanner." He cackled after them as they walked to the livery stable. "Quite a lady, is that Nancy.

And now she's Mrs Nancy Tanner."

"Let's get home! I just want to go home and sit quietly on the porch. It's getting late, but we might just make it before dark. Then we'll have peace and quiet at the ranch."

That's what Amy was hoping for. But she didn't get it!

# CHAPTER FORTY-TWO

It was a slow journey back to Broken Horseshoe Ranch as they wanted to give the horses a breather, and it gave them both time to talk.

"What's the story about the other headless corpses that have been found on the Devil's Mountain in the past?" Josh asked Amy as they rode side by side.

The sun was setting and the cacti, with their long, stilted fingers and arms, threw strange shadows across their path. The air was growing cooler and Amy told Josh that the nighttime creatures and insects would begin to make an appearance. Eager to arrive home, she fretted that they deliberately took their time to save the tired horses.

"I don't know, Josh. I've only heard that folk can get killed up there. Some have been found dying from natural causes, like a snake bite, rockfall, or if they've run out of water. But I always thought that the headless corpses were just a tall tale. That they were told to frighten rival prospectors away from the goldmines."

They rode on for a short way before Amy spoke again. "Manuel says that an old-timer told him today that there have been about three or four of them, but that was about ten years or so ago, and never since then. They never found the killer."

"Until now!" Josh said. "What do you think happened to the head? Do you think any animal would have taken it? Where did that head go?"

"I wonder if a lion took it?" Amy said thoughtfully.

"A lion? A real, honest to goodness, king of the jungle lion? No way!" The horrified expression and exclamations from Josh made Amy laugh out loud. Her peals of laughter rang out across the flat desert terrain they were travelling through.

Even Josh had to laugh with her as he continued speaking. "There are no lions living around here, are there?"

"Yes, there are a few lions said to be living up in the mountains. I've never seen one, but Ezra has seen one. He said it was huge. Luckily, Ezra said, it was as scared of him as he was of it, and it fled in one direction and he went in the other!" Amy told Josh.

"Lions! Never would I have thought that there could be a remote possibility that I could come face-to-face with a lion!" Tossing his blonde hair back from his face, his expression was still flabbergasted and it made Amy smile yet again. A companionable silence grew up between them.

A bit later, Amy spoke in a strange tone of voice. "Who wants to kill you, Josh?" She glanced at him nervously, as if frightened he might take offence at the direct question.

Josh's blue eyes, normally bright and cheerful, turned into a black-blue as he thought back to the attempt on his life. "I don't know, Amy. Riding into town today, mixing with the surrounding people, there was no one I recognised."

"Someone recognised you! And hated you so much they tried to ride you down," Amy said. The previous laughter had fled from her face and it mirrored Josh's sombre expression. "That was a deliberate attempt on your life."

"Manuel saved me. Did you know that? You were still in the general store with Eliza. Manuel saw the horse rider passed by a few people, then he deliberately picked up speed and rode his horse directly at me. I wasn't looking in that direction, and it was only Manuel's warning shout that alerted me. I flung myself to the side so avoiding him. The rider could not stop or swerve in time, and so he rode past me."

Amy spoke after a brief silence. "I wonder who it could have been. Did you see anyone looking at you suspiciously? You know, when we first arrived in town?"

"No, Amy, I thought everyone was too busy staring at our headless corpse," Josh answered her.

Silence – a dark, brooding silence – fell between them. Josh glanced across at Amy as she rode Bella beside him. She was worried about him and his safety. There could be no doubt about the fact that Amy cared for him. But was it the care you gave to a friend, or could it mean more? How Josh wished it could be more. Even if she only felt the anxious worry for a friend's safety, it still gave him a warm glow in his heart. There was never any doubt in his mind, he'd been through it again and again. He would not tell Amy how he felt about her.

Josh Barnes may not be his name. If it wasn't his name, who was he? Where did he come from? And, more to the point, what had the real him done? How could he involve a girl like Amy in a life that could explode into something that neither of them wanted or could cope with? That was what he thought before. Now, with the masked rider eager to kill him, he had tangible proof that he had been right. Someone recognised him from his past and had acted upon it.

"The masked rider spoke to me," Josh said.

Amy whirled round as far as she could on her horse to face him. "He spoke to you, Josh? Why didn't you tell me before? What did he say?"

"On realising he was going to miss me, the masked man leant forward and shouted: *'Next time*! *I'll get you next time.'*"

# CHAPTER FORTY-THREE

"Oh, no! Oh, Josh! That means you're still in danger. You are a target now. He's recognised you and is looking to kill you!" Amy exclaimed.

"What does he know about me? Why is it necessary to kill me?" Josh almost shouted the words. But asking those questions was futile. Josh knew it, but it still helped to say them out loud in the open to Amy. "Amy, who was I? What the hell did I do to merit being run down in the main street of Nowhere?"

"There is no way that you are evil! I refuse to believe it of you. All of us would know if you are a wicked man. Not one of us at the ranch thinks you are anything but good. And Meg knows you are good! She loves you!"

Josh shouted with laughter. "So I owe my good name to a dog!" He looked at Amy's indignant face. "All right! All right, Amy, I recognise Meg is a superb character witness for me. I'm very grateful to her and shall tell her so and give her a pat when we get back to the ranch."

"She should have recovered by now. That cactus spine in her paw must've been very painful. I think today will see her better," said Amy.

"Poor Meg, she looked so miserable when we left her behind today. It's just as well we didn't have her with us. It might have been difficult having her when we found his body," said Josh.

"Meg might've found his head," murmured Amy.

Josh didn't reply. He was staring in amazement at the Broken Horseshoe Ranch in the distance. Even though dusk was falling fast, they could see an enormous amount of movement, and carts and buggies drawn up outside the front of it.

Amy gave a gasp and urged on Bella to a faster pace. "What's happening now? Isn't that Nancy's buggy? What is she doing this time?"

Grinning to himself, Josh followed the irate girl surging ahead of him. Josh liked Nancy, sure she was bossy and opinionated, but she livened up those living at Broken Horseshoe Ranch. Knowing that the marriage of convenience Luke had agreed to with Nancy ensured his children would have security and someone to watch over them after his imminent death had calmed Luke's fears for the future. Luke aroused Josh's sympathy for his flu - related illness. Losing his wife in the same flu outbreak that had affected his health had been a bitter blow. Acting on the advice of a doctor, he had cut all ties with his previous city life and had brought thirteen-year-old Ben and seventeen-year-old Amy to live in a veritable wilderness. Josh found it amusing to watch Nancy manipulate Luke and felt the selfish man deserved his life to be turned upside down by the feisty widow.

"I like Nancy," Josh said, riding up to Amy as they approach the ranch. "She's good for your father, you know."

"She is? How?" Amy turned a puzzled face towards Josh.

"Nancy's got him out of that depressed state he was sinking deeper into. Your father was getting into a rut, taking little exercise, and having no interest in the ranch. She's also good with Ben. He chats to her and is no longer so quiet. Nancy isn't trying to take your mother's place, you know. She just wants to help you all in her unique, bossy fashion." It had been a long speech from Josh, and he watched as Amy took her time thinking about it.

"I get we benefit from her bossiness and her help. But, Josh, what does Nancy get out of it?"

"Nancy was frightened by Sheriff Cody. His persistence in trying to force her into marriage, I think it made her realise how alone in life she really was. She had no one who could be called upon to help her. In marrying your father, Nancy has got herself a ready-made family. She is no longer lonely and has a purpose in life bossing you lot around!"

The smile on Amy's face relieved Josh. Both Amy and Nancy were strong women. Together they would become a formidable force, but at loggerheads... Josh thought that would not be a pretty picture!

"Unpacking boxes, that's what's happening. But why? What's all that furniture doing on our porch? What's Nancy up to now?" Amy said to Josh as she rode Bella up to the porch rail, slipping down from her horse.

"Hey, Ben. What's going on here?"

"You've got to come, Amy! You've got to see this. Come and see what Nancy is doing now!"

# CHAPTER FORTY-FOUR

Josh laughed as Amy raced up the porch steps to join her brother, eager to see what Nancy had been doing.

Ezra came out to join him, taking the reins of both horses from Josh and shaking his head. "It's like a mad hornet has got into this ranch. Don't know what will come of it. Reckon that woman is stirring everything up around here. I don't like it. I don't like it at all!" The old man took both horses' reins and began leading them to the barn. "I don't like it at all. Hornet! That's what that woman is. I reckon she's a hornet."

"I don't know, Ezra, I think she's the best thing that's happened to this ranch and to the people that live here. Luke couldn't carry on like he was doing forever. It needed someone to come in and organise this family and get this ranch working properly again. Surely you can see that, Ezra? Think about it. It gives you and Leah far more security in your old age to be living on a thriving ranch."

The old man scratched his long hair and stood for a moment, thinking about Josh's words.

 Leah came around the corner, carrying a pile of freshly washed linens. "Best thing that's happened to this family. Breath of fresh air is Miss Nancy. Just what we all needed. I for one, I'm glad she's arrived. Rubbish! Ezra, you talk rubbish. You're an old fool, that's what you are. Josh is right," she scolded her husband.

Josh stepped aside, letting the old woman go past him with her load. He knew better now than to offer to help her. His offers of help had been refused on several occasions. "I'm not too old to need help from you, young man! Not too old at all," Leah had told him.

Climbing up onto the first porch step, Josh gazed

around and he could only gasp in amazement. The quiet, empty ranch house that he and Amy had left only that morning was dramatically different. There was now a tent erected beside Ezra's log cabin. A couple of buggies had furniture still piled on them, and several loads of timber had obviously been offloaded earlier. There was the chatter and laughter from men inside the tent, and a large fire in front of the tent had a large cooking pot suspended above it. The man tending the pots looked up at Josh and waved a large wooden spoon at him with a cheerful grin. Josh waved back.

"What the hell's been going on here?" he muttered and climbed the remaining porch steps and went into the cabin.

There was a tense atmosphere, and Josh realised that Amy and Nancy were the cause of it. Luke sat in his chair, a mug of coffee as usual in his hand, staring wordlessly from one to the other. Ben and Chan stood side by side in the corner, eyeing the two women warily. Only Leah was bustling around, ignoring the drama unfolding around her.

Nancy and Amy had squared off in front of each other.

The older woman, for the first time since Josh had met her, looked nervous. "Now, Amy, don't get mad at me. Your Pa is on his own, fretting over you and your safety when you're out on your own searching for the treasure. He doesn't eat properly, he doesn't do the right sort of movements to keep him fit. I told you before that I didn't want to be no widow again. So I'm moving into the ranch. I'm going to make this ranch bigger and better. Miguel's wife is expecting another baby so they can move into my place. They need more room and it's bigger for them. The tent outside is for my men to stay while they build extra rooms onto this ranch house, another bedroom for you, Ben, and myself, and a proper sitting room." Nancy ran out of breath.

The entire room fell silent as each person stared at Amy, wondering what she would say or do. It was a pivotal moment in all their lives, Josh thought, and like everyone else, he wondered how the girl would react towards the older woman and her ideas for changing, not only the ranch house, but all their lives. As he watched her, Amy glanced towards him, and he saw her eyes widen and a growing awareness filled them and she nodded to him. Josh wondered what that nod meant.

What was Amy going to do?

# CHAPTER FORTY-FIVE

Amy gave Josh a brief smile, and she took a step forward to the older woman. "Thank you, Nancy!" Amy said and flung her arms around Nancy, giving her a hug.

Nancy's eyes filled with tears, and she hugged Amy back, trying to wipe the tears away so that no one would notice.

It was Leah who interrupted the emotional scene, bringing them all back to earth. "I've got a pot of chilli on the stove and fresh made biscuits. Ben and Chan, come and get them, and all you folks settle down for a meal. I, for one, am right glad you've arrived here, Mrs Nancy. You're a breath of fresh air, and just what we all needed."

"What's wrong, Amy? What's happened today?" Luke had seen something in his daughter's face that had alerted him to the fact that all was not well with her.

Amy turned to Josh, and the words flooded out from her. "You tell them! It's horrible, Pa. I don't want to talk about it. I'll go and wash up, ready for my chilli." Amy almost ran out of the room, eager to leave the telling of the tale to Josh.

It took a while before Amy returned. Josh thought she must've sat out on the porch waiting until he had told the story, and they had all commented on it. On her re-entry through the door, Josh gave her a smiling nod and Amy cast him a grateful glance before sitting down at the table.

"How terrible for both of you," said Nancy. "I've heard the tales about these murders happening in the past years. But there's never been one in all the time I've been living here. What about you, Ezra? You've lived here a long time. Do you remember any of the headless corpse murders?"

Ezra shook his head, the flowing white locks of his hair springing into life as he did so. "Heard tell of many folks getting killed. Some were lost in the mountains, and the tales of their deaths were downright fanciful. Never believed the stories about the headless corpses, but here we are, with one on our doorstep!"

Hardly on the doorstep, thought Josh. He thought of the long, arduous journey with the body on Bella's back. That had been no brief trip. The body they had found was certainly not on the doorstep. But he, too, wondered at this re-emergence of the headless body murders.

"You did your Christian duty by the body? Said a prayer over him?" Luke directed the question at Amy. When she nodded, Luke continued speaking. "Strange as it is, surely it must be a murder committed to gain the old boy's stash of gold or silver. The beheading must be done to get everyone's attention away from a simple attack of greed. Also, it perpetuates the headless body legend of the Devil's Mountain. But I can't understand why anyone would want to continue with these decapitations!"

Ezra left as Ben and Chan came in with the chilli and the biscuits. There was a silence of appreciation whilst eating Leah's cooking. Nancy, Luke, Amy, and Josh sat at the table. The boys sat together on a bench beneath the window with their plates on their knees.

When the last mouthful had been eaten and Ben had got the last biscuit as usual, Nancy began speaking. She sat back with an empty plate in front of her. "That Leah is a splendid cook. I'm really pleased she's been good enough to include me in her evening meals." Nancy scratched her bun, and more tendrils of hair escaped. "Useless in the kitchen, that's me! When it comes to cooking, I'm hopeless. I've tried. I tried hard when we first got wed. Somehow, I could never get the timing right. Either my stew would burn or the biscuits would. Nothing would ever cook right together."

Amy smiled in sympathy. She wasn't very successful at the stove either. Impatient at her daily burnt offerings, Chan had declared, in an act of desperation, that he was going to take over the cooking. His splendid success at cooking delicious meals out of whatever was available had Amy agreeing wholeheartedly to giving up her cooking chores.

Amy turned to Josh. "Have you told them about the masked rider?"

"What masked rider?" Luke leant forward over the table, his gaze alert as he looked at the younger man.

Josh turned to Amy. "I think you can tell this story."

Amy looked round at the eager faces. "Well, I was in the general store with Eliza before coming back to the ranch. Whilst there, I took the opportunity to get a few more provisions. Josh was walking down to get the horses from the livery stables. Manuel had walked out of the store to chat with him and Manuel stood there as Josh walked down Main Street." Amy paused for breath, then swallowed hard.

She was finding it hard to continue with the story. To remember how near to death Josh had come left her emotionally drained. She had realised that he meant so much more to her than just a casual stranger. It had become so important to her life that Josh remained a part of it. When he had lain face down in the dirt with that horse galloping past him, her heart had betrayed the thoughts that she had been trying to convince herself were not present within it. The realisation of just how much Josh meant to her was frightening, as she felt the situation they were living in could not accommodate the feelings that she now held. However much she felt this overwhelming love for Josh, it must remain hidden. No one, especially Josh, need ever know how she felt about him.

Josh took over the story. "There's a new storefront being built, and I was looking at it to find out what it was going to sell. Then I heard Manuel shout at me. He alerted me to a rider who was coming down Main Street. This horseman was picking up speed and avoiding other folk on the road. He was heading straight for me! At Manuel's shout, I saw him just in the nick of time. I flung myself to one side and out of his way."

"Oh my! You could have been killed. What an escape you had!" Nancy exclaimed.

"You didn't see his face at all?" Luke asked, a frown creasing his forehead.

"No, he had his hat pulled down low and the lower half of his face was hidden behind a red scarf with white spots pulled up over it," Josh replied.

Amy pushed her plate away, settled back in her chair, and spoke. "Tell them, Josh, tell them what the man said to you," Amy urged him.

Slightly wavering, Josh's voice was harsh as he repeated the masked rider's words. "He bent down from his horse and said, '*Next time. I'll get you next time!*'"

It was Luke who broke the silence. "Someone recognised you, Josh, and tried to kill you. You've always wondered if you were a killer. No need to wonder anymore. You're no killer. Someone is looking for you to kill you. I think they thought you were dead when they left you in the desert, when Amy found you. No, Josh, you're not a murderer. You're the victim!"

# CHAPTER FORTY-SIX

Ben said what everyone had been thinking. "Why would someone want to kill you?"

"I don't know, Ben. Do you know how infuriating and frustrating it is to have nothing but blackness where your memory should be? I see a drink, or even the rain, and wonder did I like it? Where have I been? Where did I come from?" The words spewed out in a torrent. Josh's angry frustration had reached a boiling point within him.

"And!" He repeated the word with even greater emphasis. "And, the one and only person who has recognised me, tried to kill me! Do you know how galling that is? He rode past me! He knew who I was and what my past was, and he not only rode past me, but he also tried to kill me!" Josh's words rang out around the cabin. His frustrated anger was obvious to all. Then, overcome with the day's events, he dropped his head into his hands. The tousled blonde hair flopped around his hands, and his shoulders slumped in an attitude of abject dejection.

Nancy looked at Amy, who half rose from her chair, eager to comfort Josh. Nancy shook her head and mouthed the words to Amy. "Leave him be."

Amy nodded and sank back down onto her chair, her face full of sympathy and her hands clasping and unclasping in distress.

"Pain is an evil thing, and it is difficult to accept and cope with it. But helpless frustration at life, at unbidden and unexpected experiences, can be painful in a different way. It grows and claws at the heart and mind. I can't advise you how to cope with it, Josh. I'm still looking for answers for myself, so I can sympathise with you wholeheartedly," Luke said to Josh. The older man's face was solemn, and the wrinkles deepened as he talked. Lines of pain had been etched in his face, a few from the disease that now had him in its grip, but most were from grief at his wife's death and the difficulties his illness had brought to their lives.

Josh lifted his head and looked at the older man. Luke continued speaking. "However, I can ask you all to pray together. Let us pray for the repose of the soul of the murdered man. Let us pray for our new life together with Nancy, Chan, and Josh. Lord God, you have brought us together in a new family at Broken Horseshoe Ranch. Look down on us this night. Thank you for the deliverance of these two young people today. Keep us all safe and secure in Your hands throughout this night and the days ahead."

Heads were bowed, and Amens fervently said. A peace descended on the cabin, and it was broken only by the necessity of sorting out their sleeping arrangements. It took some doing, but finally everyone had a place to sleep. As the final arrangements were made, the bedding was placed in its usual corner of the cabin. Chan and Ben plonked themselves down together, but leaving Josh the greater part of the quilts. Suddenly, in the quiet of the evening, the sound of galloping hooves could be heard.

"A rider! Who can it be at this time of night?" Luke exclaimed, and he walked out of the door to stand on the porch. The night was clear, with the moon shining on the landscape, the desert stretching out before the ranch. Cacti cast eerie shapes whilst boulders and rocks hid purple shadows. Behind the ranch, the mountains with the peak of the Devil's Mountain looked sinister as they overshadowed everything. Moonlight turned the rock faces a steely grey-blue, whilst the crevices and canyons hid in forbidding blackness.

The porch became crowded as everyone gathered to see who it was that was galloping at such a pace. The men had their rifles and guns at the ready. Anyone coming at this time of night was suspect. There were many who roamed around seeking to rob the unwary householder.

"Hello, Luke! Hello, Nancy! It's Ramon, I've come with news!"

Chan and Ben ran down to stand at the bottom step, ready to be the first to greet the newcomer and take his horse.

Ramon rode his horse up to the cabin porch steps and handed the reins to Ben. Ramon was the son of Manuel and Eliza from the general store. He jumped down and rushed up to them. "Pa sent me to warn you. There's been another one! Another silver prospector who worked over by the old Indian silver mines, the other side of Devil's Mountain, has also been found headless. All his equipment, his horse, and everything is still there. Someone came up real close to him, killed him, and then..." Here the young boy drew a finger across his neck in a manner to show decapitation.

"Come on in. Let's get you a drink and your horse stabled," said Luke. "You're not riding back tonight with such a madman roaming about."

Josh smiled at the relief on the young Mexican's face. He'd hoped for an offer to stay the night but had been preparing himself for the dangerous journey back if no offer had been forthcoming.

"A bowl of chilli and some of Leah's biscuits, and then you can bed down with my men in the tent tonight," said Nancy, ushering the young boy into the cabin.

With his hat in his hand, Ramon climbed the steps and came in to sit down at the table. The young man took after his father, with a dark, swarthy complexion, the coal black hair and the deep brown eyes. But when he smiled, it was his mother's cheerful countenance that could be seen in him.

"Oh! I forgot! Josh, my father gave me a special message for you. That rider who tried to knock you down today was asking about you around Nowhere earlier. He asked about a yellow-haired man called Josh Barnes, who spoke in a funny English accent. The saloon keeper told him who you were, and even took him to the door and pointed you out. Pa was angry about that, said the saloon keeper should have minded his own business."

"You were a target," said Nancy.

"He was looking for you," said Ezra.

"Someone is looking for you, to kill you," Luke said.

These comments from everyone came at once. Not one person present had not been outraged by this additional news from Manuel. There was a general hubbub of indignation and surprised worry over this fresh development, concerning the attack upon Josh in Nowhere that morning.

Ramon took no part in this conversation. He was too intent on devouring the chilli and biscuits.

The silence was heavy in the room. This new knowledge about Josh was something to consider. It affected Josh and what he felt about himself, but it also affected the others in the room. If Josh was not an American but an Englishman, it turned him into a different person who had come to America for some compelling reason. What was that reason? That was the question foremost in everyone's thoughts, most especially the thoughts of Josh himself.

"Josh! Now we know that's why you speak so funny! You're English, and that's an English accent," cried Ben in excitement. "Why did you leave England? What brought you to America? Why are you here at Broken Horseshoe Ranch?"

# CHAPTER FORTY-SEVEN

It was Nancy who stood up and spoke into the quiet that had suddenly descended. All eyes had gone to Josh. Not only was Josh distraught, but he was also puzzled. But Nancy was having no more emotional scenes tonight. She'd had her fill of them today. No more. It was the usual time for Nancy to step outside on the porch and have her last cheroot of the day. It had been a habit that she'd picked up from her husband. Finding packets of them in his desk after his death, she had smoked one of them and developed a liking for them. But not tonight. There was no way Nancy could produce her bad habit into the turmoil of this evening!

"Ezra, please take the boy and settle him and his horse down for the night. Ben and Chan, your bedding is sorted out. Both of you and Josh get some sleep. Luke and Amy, go to your bedrooms and go to sleep as well." Her sharp tones gave them no excuse to argue with her. Everyone carried out her orders immediately. "Oh, Amy, I put a bedroll in beside you for tonight. We'll get to work building other rooms tomorrow. Oh, and Ezra..."

"Way ahead of you, Miss Nancy. I'll get a guard posted, and the lads will take turns during the night to watch."

"Well done. You're a good man, Ezra, and sharp as well." Nancy's words were said in her usual brisk fashion, but they were just what Ezra needed, Josh thought. Ezra was a quiet man and her words of praise ignited a loyalty in the old man that boded well for future life at Broken Horseshoe Ranch.

Sometime later, Amy and Nancy had retired to the newspaper wall cupboard bedroom. Josh had been amused at Amy's face at the intrusion of the older woman – first into her life, and now her sleeping quarters. So many times he saw Amy look down at the ground, and visibly bite her lip to prevent the comments that she was itching to make. Impressed by her self-restraint in what was a difficult situation for the girl, Josh realised that she'd taken to heart the words of advice from Eliza, the Preacher, and even himself.

"Josh. I'm going to have a whiskey on the porch. Care to join me?" Luke stood with the bottle in his hand and two tin cups already out on the table. His disobedience of his new wife's orders had given the older man the look of an errant schoolboy.

"Is that an invitation or a summons?" Josh said, his smile at the older man taking the sting out of the words. He slipped from the quilts on the floor, taking care not to wake the boys.

"Bit of both, I reckon," Luke said, his weary eyes glinting with amusement.

"Here! Take this, reckon you deserve it. You've had one helluva day, one way or another." Luke opened the door and stepped out onto the porch, shivering a little as the cooling air hit his frail body.

Knowing any comment would be rebuffed, Josh sat down with a sigh. He sipped the whiskey, letting the warm liquid swirl about his mouth. A swallow, and the heat swept through his body. Josh sighed again, this time not from weariness but from sheer pleasure. Stretching his long legs out, he lent back against the cabin wall, the tension in his shoulders easing.

"That accent of yours must be English," Luke said. "Thought you were an Easterner, not much to choose between the voices sometimes. That fellow must've been told to look out for you. Someone knows who you are, and they are looking for you."

Running his hand through his hair, Josh spoke. "I've lain awake, night after night, trying to remember places, people, even things that I might have used. Nothing! When Amy found me, for the first few days after that, there were flashes, strange pictures, and wispy glimpses of places. Never people. I never once saw a person," said Josh.

"And now?" prompted Luke.

"Now, there's only a complete blankness. Even those glimpses don't come any more."

"Danger is now stalking you, Josh. There is a man somewhere with a vicious streak out to kill. Great care must be taken by all of us, not only to watch out for your masked rider but also for the madman out beheading folk. There is a terrible world of violence that is malevolent and evil and now prowls about the Devil's Mountain. Yes, the malevolence stalks Devil's Mountain this very night."

The night sky was illuminated by the full moon, but its luminosity did not eclipse the brightness of the hundreds of stars. For a while, the two men sat in a companionable silence, relishing the peace that comes at the end of the day, especially at the end of a tumultuous, heat-soaked day.

"Yet I know things, Luke. Somehow, I know that I have never experienced the silence of the night sky and the wonder of it in the desert. It's an overwhelming experience."

"It is special, Josh. Every night I come out to enjoy this. It grounds me in the reality and futility of life as we know it. My God becomes closer and I can send my prayers skyward, whilst thanking Him for this majestic spectacle."

Again, they sat in silence. There was nothing more to be said, and nothing needed to be said between them. The two men understood each other and respected each other.

"Take Ezra with you tomorrow, Josh. There needs to be more of you on alert when you go up in the foothills of the Devil's Mountain now. Everything out here either bites, stings, or has poisonous prickles. Now you have a masked rider gunning for you, and a man filled with such malevolence towards his fellow humans that not only does he kill them, but he also decapitates them!"

Luke stood up and walked to the cabin door. "Josh, look out for yourself and my daughter. The Devil's Mountain is now filled with malevolence. Don't let the Devil get you!"

# CHAPTER FORTY-EIGHT

Chan was cooking breakfast as usual. Ben was out seeing to the horses. A sleepy Amy appeared, following Nancy, who was tucking her hair up into her bun. Josh was surprised to see the older woman, fresh, enthusiastic, and tidy, verging on smartness. Today, Nancy had opted for trousers, large canvas ones which she turned up at the ankles, obviously made for a larger man. Men's boots – even larger sized than those worn by Amy – a man's plaid shirt, and a cotton jacket completed her outfit. Struggling to hold back his laughter, Josh looked away from Amy.

"Pleasant night's sleep, despite being on my bedroll, hope to be in my proper bed tonight, or at the very latest tomorrow night," Nancy said, rubbing her hands enthusiastically.

Chan dished out the meal with pride, and they all sat down to enjoy it.

"Well cooked, Chan, you are becoming a skilled chef. I'm looking forward to having this each morning!" Nancy said, rising from the table. She gave Chan a hearty, encouraging slap on the back.

This time, it was both Josh and Amy who had to hide their smiles as Chan, a slight boy, was sent flying at this friendly blow. Only Josh's outstretched arm prevented his fall. But the boy beamed with pleasure at Nancy's remarks.

Nancy stomped out of the cabin and down the steps, calling out for her men.

"She's so bossy and loud, but she's so kind-hearted, even her men respect and love her," Amy whispered to Josh.

Chan nodded. "Very kind lady, very kind indeed," he

said. His face was beaming with pride at the kindly words Nancy had said to him. Insignificant praise, yet it meant so much to the small boy who had been so badly treated in his earlier life.

"Your Pa wants Ezra to come with us today, Amy. He's worried about our safety," Josh said.

"Good idea, Ezra is so experienced in this desert and mountain country, I'll swear he can smell danger. Meg is eager to join us, too. But her paw hasn't healed yet. She'll have to stay behind yet again," Amy said as she got her coat, gun, and hat. She looked slightly dishevelled, even her plaits were lopsided this morning.

"Bad night?" Josh enquired.

Amy glanced around to make certain that Nancy was out of earshot, before whispering to Josh. "She snores and talks in her sleep. I kept drifting off and then waking up at another loud snore from her."

"Never mind, Nancy said it wouldn't be for long," Josh sympathised.

Ben had the horses ready. But before they could leave, Chan rushed out with a parcel for Amy. They had filled their water bottles earlier, and Amy had taken some hard biscuits.

"What's this, Chan?" Amy asked the boy, as she took the parcel to put in her saddlebag.

"Mrs Nancy sent me to give you a lunch. You need good food to keep a sharp lookout, she says." A broad grin came from Chan at their astonished faces as he ran off to see if Mrs Nancy had anything else for him to do.

Amy shook her head and stowed the parcel away. "I shall thank her later."

This life he was living was interesting and Josh found himself enjoying it. The advent of Nancy at the ranch was going to liven them all up. A lady who congratulates an insignificant Chinese boy on his cooking and, during her building works, can remember to give her new stepdaughter lunch for her day's journey, was someone special.

"Tell me more about this sign and the symbol. Where did you find it?" Ezra asked them as they rode along.

They told Ezra all that they remembered. He nodded, knowing the area well, yet surprised that he'd never seen the signs for himself.

Ezra spoke sadly. "You said that the beheaded body was old Bert. I remember him. Years ago he arrived here, dead set on finding the silver mine and getting a fortune. He wanted to go back home, wherever that was, and show them what a big man he had become. Strange man, but harmless enough, didn't deserve that way of dying," Ezra said, shaking his head.

The cool of the morning was disappearing fast, and the heat was becoming unbearable as the sun rose in the sky. The sun's rays began to rebound from the rocks and the canyon walls which rose above them. All of them began to sweat and wipe their brows as the heat and glare of the sun grew more intense.

"Time for a rest in the shade," Ezra called to them, and set off towards some tall boulders. The other two followed him. They gave the horses some water and settled themselves against the cooler, shaded rock. Amy opened the parcel Nancy gave her. There were some biscuits left over from breakfast, along with some slices of cold ham. Pulling out the hard biscuits she had brought, Amy asked what the men preferred.

"Go on, choose. I'm having Nancy's kind offering. There's enough for the three of us, but take the hard biscuits if you prefer them."

There was no reply, but both men reached out to take Nancy's tastier and fresher lunch.

After eating and having some water, they made ready to continue their trek. Standing up, brushing down their clothes, all three climbed back on their horses.

"Let's try to make that last sign before it gets too hot," said Amy.

"That's where you found that fellow, near to that sign?" Ezra asked.

"Yes," said Amy, turning to follow Josh as he led the way towards the foothills of the Devil's Mountain.

A sudden noise of thundering hooves racing towards them had them all stopping and turning to face the oncoming rider.

# CHAPTER FORTY-NINE

"Hello there, Gabe! How are you doing?" Ezra shouted as the ageing prospector rode up to them.

"What are you doing out here? Are you looking for those goldmines? They're all mine now. The Thunder God says they belong to me. Do you hear me? They all belong to me? All the gold is mine now! The Thunder God told me," Gabe shouted at them as he came closer.

"No, no, we're not prospecting at all, Gabe," Ezra's measured tones were meant to soothe the older man. "No, we're not looking for a mine."

"What are you doing this way out here, then? Tell me that! What are you doing out here?" shouted the old man at them. Hairy eyebrows knitted together in a ferocious frown and the straggly beard jerked up and down with his shouted words.

Josh noted the man's unkempt clothes. His coarse, woollen trousers were covered in brown stains, his jacket was torn and hung awkwardly on him. He'd obviously lost weight and his clothes no longer fitted him. The old man kept darting suspicious looks at each one of them as he fingered the rifle in one hand.

"This here Englishmen never been to Devil's Mountain before. Going to take him up the canyon so that he can see the mountains close to," was Ezra's quick reply.

"English ha! That lot is as bad as those damn Yankees. No time for any of them." With that, Gabe held his rifle in a tighter grip, and raised it up, pointing it at Josh.

"Don't you worry about Josh here, Gabe. He is a harmless lad. He's a bit simple, like, doesn't remember things." Ezra's voice held a panicky note, which didn't escape Josh. He wondered if he should fling himself off his horse, away from the gun that was pointing straight at his heart.

"There's three of you," said Gabe. All of a sudden, he seemed to notice Amy. He stared fixedly at her before speaking to her. "You're a girl! What are you doing out here?" Slowly, the rifle was lowered, but he didn't put it away. It lay handy enough in his hands. "Ha. It's no good if there are three of them, and one of them a girl." At this strange remark, he rode off as suddenly as he had appeared.

"That's strange. Never knew old Gabe to act like that. Always a loner, kept himself to himself. He hardly spoke to anyone when he came into Nowhere for supplies. But Gabe usually had a civil time of day for everyone. Even if it was brief. Never had this strange talk of the Thunder God, though," said Ezra. The older man shook his head, a puzzled frown upon his face as he looked after the disappearing Gabe.

"I thought he was going to shoot you, Josh." Amy shuddered at the remembrance of that rifle pointed towards Josh and the weird look in Gabe's eyes. "What was all that talk about the Thunder God, Ezra? What do you think he meant by it?"

"I don't know. I think he's been on his own too long in the mountains. They sometimes affect a fellow. The mountains, the loneliness, and the heat of the day can make them act strange," Ezra said.

Josh nodded at the other man. "I can believe it, Ezra. These mountains have a strange atmosphere which only gets stronger the further you go into them. As you say, Ezra, it could easily drive a man into madness."

They rode on, but an uneasiness rode alongside them.

Gabe's peculiar reactions to their presence in the mountains had unnerved them all. Their wariness because of the masked rider and the beheaded bodies was now heightened to such a level that they constantly searched their surroundings as they rode on.

"It's not far now, Ezra, that ledge up there is where we sheltered during the storm. Josh found the first sign and number along that far ledge. We were waiting after the storm, just like you told me to, in case of any flash floods," said Amy.

Josh looked at Ezra and smiled at the older man. "I confess I didn't believe Amy about the floods. But it was a terrifying experience seeing that wall of water rush down the canyon. The way boulders and trees were tossed around in the maelstrom of water was..." Words failed Josh, but both Amy and Ezra nodded in agreement.

In a short time, they reached the last sign. It was pointed out to Ezra, along with the place that Bert's body had been found. Tethering the horses, they climbed up between enormous boulders and over pebbly shingle patches, each more difficult to cope with than the last one.

"There is no number on this one," said Amy. She pointed to the symbol carved on the rock.

"Yes, there's only a Jesuit cross and an arrow pointing into the rock face at the end of the canyon," Ezra said. He turned towards the direction in which the arrow pointed. He screwed up his ageing eyes against the glare of the sun. "Look up there! I see a few more crevices in the rock face. The sun has caught them as it's shining straight at the rock face. Normally you'd never see them. Let's have a look. Come on, this is interesting." They rode further along the canyon to tether the horses again, this time making certain they were in shade because of the increasing heat.

Josh felt a rising excitement within him. He could see both Ezra and Amy were also as eager and excited as he was, now they were following up on this latest clue. Josh reached the first vertical cliff face with the crevice-like cave opening. It had been a tough climb, although not very high up. The ledge they climbed on was scattered with rubble and stones from various cliff falls in the past. Stepping over them, Josh clambered to the opening of the cave. Looking in it, he could see through the narrow opening a level floor opening out to a much larger area that sloped downwards.

"Don't go in! Step away from it now, Josh. Don't move!"

# CHAPTER FIFTY

Racing up as fast as he could, Ezra had reached Josh and grabbed him by the arm, pulling him back. "No, Josh! You mustn't go in, it could be booby-trapped." The old man dragged Josh back from the cave entrance before he finally released that iron grip on his arm.

"Booby-trapped? Why? Who would have done that?" Josh had followed Ezra further back from the cave entrance and could only stare in amazement at the old man and his urgent commands.

"It's common knowledge. Old-timers tell of booby-trapped mines where caches of gold, silver, and bullion may have been hidden. They put traps in place to kill anyone who might come and steal it," Ezra answered him.

"It looks untouched and innocent of anything dangerous," said Josh.

"All the better to trap the unwary," said Ezra. The old man stood well back from the cave entrance, then walked up and down in front of it. His long white hair was ruffled by the breeze that blew in wild, hot gusts around them. Although it was cooler now, as they were further up and into the mountains, the wind carried the heat from the desert plains below.

"Look at these, Josh. See, the flat ledge goes into the cave entrance."

"Yes, Ezra, it slopes down and is a continuation of the rock face on which we are standing," Josh said as he and Amy peered around Ezra and followed his pointing finger with intent looks.

"But there is a patch of rough gravel and rocks before the rock floor continues. See that?" The old man's gnarled finger with its grimy nail pointed yet again.

"Yes," they replied. Both of them peered round Ezra again and scrutinised the area Ezra was telling them about.

"Josh, grab the heaviest boulder you can carry and throw it in there to land in the middle of that gravelly patch. Then we all run as far back as we can. And as fast as we can!"

Not one of them could ever relate exactly what happened next. The boulder that Josh threw landed on the gravelly patch just where Ezra had told him to aim for. When the boulder hit the patch, a flurry of stones flew up in the air before falling into a rapidly opening abyss. The gravel patch fell away into nothingness. There was a loud grinding, clinking noise as the sides of the cave opening fell onto the cave floor and fell into the hole opening up beneath them. Rocks fell from the cave roof, from the cave sides, and thundered down into the opening hole that had been beneath the gravel.

"Best get back!" Ezra urged them. "Get back now, well away from the cave." Ezra's voice was harsh and panicky again. It galvanised both Josh and Amy into action.

They rushed back along the ledge, standing at a safe distance from the cave mouth. Dust billowed out in huge clouds. Rocks and boulders fell from the roof of the cave and rolled out of the actual cave entrance. Some of the heavier rocks and boulders had enough momentum to career across the rock ledge exactly to where they'd been standing. These finally hurtled down to the canyon floor. The noise was deafening. The sound of rocks crashing onto the cave floor, out onto the ledge, and then onto the canyon floor echoed around the canyon walls.

"Ezra, without you today we would be dead for sure!" Amy said, and threw her arms around the old man and hugged him.

A delighted grin spread across the old man's face, almost breaking it in two. "Seems a body may get old but can still have their uses after all."

"You said it, Ezra. You most certainly have your uses. Thank you for saving my life. Without you grabbing my arm, I would have walked in there," Josh said, looking back at the tumbled pile of rocks under which he would have been buried.

"Let's get a drink and think about what we do next," said Amy, leading the way down to the canyon floor.

The fallen boulders and gravelly stones that came from the cave fall lay around them. Thankfully, they had left the horses in the shade, which had been well away from the fall.

"What now, Ezra?" Josh asked him as all three stared up at the cliff face and its avalanche of rocks.

"Look, the sun has moved around now. It's shining straight into the cave. I suggest we go up there and take another look and see what damage has been done to the entrance."

Despite his age, it was Ezra who led the way up, nimbly avoiding the debris from the fall. It seemed only a short time before they once again stood on the cliff ledge. Cautiously, Ezra made his way to the open mouth of the cave. Rocks lay strewn about the ledge, some still at the cave mouth itself. The three of them stood silent, aghast at the devastation wrought by the throw of one single large boulder.

"We could have been under that," whispered Amy. Her face was white, and she was biting nervously at her nail.

"Thanks seems so inadequate, Ezra. When I look at what would have happened if you hadn't grabbed my arm," Josh said, words failing him as he looked again at the debris. The old man smiled at him and shrugged his shoulders before wandering further along the ledge.

"Josh, Amy, come round here! Come and look at this!"

# CHAPTER FIFTY-ONE

"There's a cross on that wall! Just a plain cross. Nothing else, no numbers. That means this is an important site. There may well be something hidden in this cave." Ezra had a glint in his eyes, and there was an excitement creeping into his voice as his fingers stroked his straggly beard. The cross was set within a square and had shaped ends and had been carved with great care. There had been a definite purpose in carving the symbol. Josh wondered if they could decipher it.

Josh looked at the old man. Could it be that Ezra now felt that they were actually on the path to some treasure? "You think this is an important clue?"

"Yes, Josh, it's definitely worth investigating further. We'll go back to the ranch and return at first light with some tools. An important clue? Yes, I think it is," Ezra said.

"Who do you think made the booby-trap, Ezra?" Amy asked as they prepared to mount their horses. "Do you think it was Jesuits or Indians? Or perhaps the old original miners?"

Ezra stood beside his horse, thinking about Amy's words. His shaggy eyebrows knit together in an effort to answer Amy's question. Scratching his head, he turned and looked up at the cave mouth, and the devastation caused by the booby-trap before speaking. "I think it's got to be the old miners or the Jesuits, Amy. That rockfall had knowledge behind it. The Indian booby-traps I've seen are more straightforward, not so complicated, but just as deadly, if not more so."

"That much work and determination to keep people out of the cave must mean that there is a treasure hidden in there that is worth hiding," said Josh. The eagerness that he felt was clear in his voice. Josh now wanted to investigate the cave and its secrets further. He couldn't wait to get in there and hunt for the treasure.

"Maybe," said Ezra, now mounted on his horse and riding alongside Josh. "Maybe not, Josh. You have to remember those Jesuits had a name for cunning and intrigue. A booby-trap in a mine with nothing in it would be their idea of a joke. So don't get your hopes up too high," Ezra warned Josh.

Was Ezra really warning Josh? He was not so sure. That warning could have applied equally to Ezra and to himself. Josh had detected a slight glint of gold fever, even in that most practical and sceptical of men. Ezra wanted to go back and look for gold. He was just as keen as Josh to look for the treasure.

The rest of the journey back to Broken Horseshoe Ranch passed in silence. Each one of them had plenty to think about. Josh saw Amy was in a pensive mood and occasionally her hand would go to her mouth. She nibbled on a nail and, suddenly realising what she was doing, her hand would be flung away. Amy's constant battle over biting her nails, Josh thought, was a truly unique feminine trait that she showed. He never commented on it, but it amused him as he watched her.

Sometime later, Ezra called a halt, and they stood in the shade of a couple of saguaro cacti. A sip of water and a stretch of their legs broke the journey in the increasing heat of the day.

"I wonder what Nancy will have got up to today?" Amy said as she put her water bottle back on her horse. "Every time I return from the day's search, she has started a new project or dismantled something."

"That lady is always busy. She has a head teeming with new ideas. She sure loves sorting folk out, and telling them what to do," Ezra chuckled.

"It is always for everyone's benefit. She always means well," Josh said, looking at Amy as he spoke. "I think Luke is looking better, and he has more energy now."

Ezra gave a hearty guffaw. "Yes, Josh, Luke doesn't sit all day moping about. That Miss Nancy tells him in no uncertain terms to get off his backside! And he does, and it's doing him the world of good."

Josh saw a pensive look cross Amy's face. Good, he thought, she's beginning to realise that Nancy is a good person and maybe a valuable asset in keeping her father alive for much longer than he would without her entrance into their lives.

Sometime later, they passed the large cactus and came to the fork in the trail. The left branch led round to the other side of Devil's Mountain. They approached the junction and turned off for home. Then, a shot came from behind some rocks!

# CHAPTER FIFTY-TWO

The first shot came from behind some rocks. Ezra drew in a sharp breath and fell off his horse, landing heavily in the dirt. A cloud of dust rose up around him as his body flattened onto the earth. His horse, an old, reliable one, stood still, looking down at Ezra and awaiting further instructions from him.

Amy screamed and threw herself off her horse to rush towards Ezra. Josh jumped from his horse as well and grabbed the reins of Amy's horse, leading them both behind some boulders.

"No, Amy! Leave Ezra, get into cover, we must hide!" Josh shouted to the girl. He grabbed Amy by the arm and pulled her back to join himself and the horses. "You'll get killed trying to reach Ezra. We must find safety for ourselves or we'll be no help for Ezra."

"Nowhere to hide!" The voice came from behind the largest of the group of boulders beside them. "Nowhere to hide! Now I'm going to kill you, Josh Barnes."

When they had set off that morning, they little thought that they would be ambushed and facing death for the second time that day. Today's journey was going to be a straightforward ride to the giant cactus with the intriguing marks carved into it, and then on up the canyon to see this last symbol, or so they had thought. Exiting the canyon, they had proceeded on their way home beneath the cliff walls, which grew taller and more jagged as the canyon itself grew narrower and wound its way around the Devil's Mountain before reaching the desert plains.

An ideal spot for an ambush, thought Josh, as he grabbed Amy's arm and tried to pull her further into cover, away from the gunfire and that gloating voice.

"Don't move! Don't try to draw your gun or I'll kill you. Come forward, both of you. I need to see your faces. Got to be sure I have the right man. Else I don't get my money."

The mocking voice and the words that he spoke chilled both Amy and Josh, despite the rising heat of the day. Both moved forward, turning slightly to face the man who emerged from behind a large rock.

"That's better. I can see your faces now." Tall, with long, black hair that straggled over a black shirt, his black trousers ended in a pair of black boots with silver embossing. He stood motionless in the shadows. Blinking in the direct glare of the sun, they were at a disadvantage. Overpowering menace flowed from the dark figure. The rifle he held in his hand moved slightly as he focused and aimed it at Amy.

The masked rider stepped forward out of the shadows and into the sunlight and Josh exclaimed. "You! You were the one who tried to run me down in Nowhere!" The man in black was now in the direct sun, and they could see he was wearing a bright red bandanna with white spots. His eyes glittered with cold, calculating malice.

"What a shame I missed you! I won't miss this time. There are no Mexicans here to give you an early warning," was the harsh reply.

"Come here, girl, I don't want to shoot you by mistake, do I?" He looked Amy up and down, making her feel unclean. Amy shifted restlessly under that gaze and moved closer to Josh.

Josh's grip on Amy's arm tightened, and neither of them moved.

"Now!" The word was barked at Amy as his echoing shot rang out around the canyon. Dust flew up at her feet as the bullet barely missed her foot. "Now!" This time, the word was hissed, but the evil intent behind it caused shivers to run up and down Amy's spine.

"Go on. Do as he says," Josh said. The words came out through his gritted teeth, his jaw already aching from clenching them in useless fury. There had to be a way out of this. Somehow, he, Amy, and Ezra couldn't die here in a useless situation. Who was this man? Why did he want to kill him? What had this Josh Barnes done to merit being hunted down to be killed like an animal? How could he let Amy be taken? Wild thoughts chased each other through his mind, around and around. But all Josh could do was watch helplessly.

Amy walked slowly towards the man. He was larger than her, stockily built, with broad shoulders and muscular arms. The dark garments he wore added to the powerful air of menace that exuded from him. His eyes again swept over her body, and he smiled. That smile from him turned Amy's stomach into cold icicles of fear. There was nothing he needed to say. That look from him told Amy of his intentions towards her. Fear overwhelmed her. His hand was large, with black hair growing down from his wrist. He reached out and fastened his hand on her wrist, yanking her arm and pulling her closer to him, but slightly behind, making certain that she was not blocking his view of Josh. A stench from him almost made her gag. Whiskey and tobacco fought with the smell of his acrid sweat. Amy had been frightened before. On many occasions, she had fought the fear and managed to overcome the frightening prospect before her. Somehow, this was different. She looked at Josh, at the impotent anger that was so clear on his face. Amy could see his hands clenching, the knuckles white. She took a deep breath and tried to push the fear away. There had to be some way out of this. There had to be! The prospect of being helpless in the hands of this man whose present touch upon her wrist was ruthless was not to be thought of. Those eyes of his had promised more of the same, very much more!

# CHAPTER FIFTY-THREE

Amy could feel the bruise forming on her wrist from the man's cruel grip. She ignored the pain. Far greater was the fear of what was to come from him. That thought left her feeling sick and powerless.

Glancing back along the canyon towards Ezra, her heart sank as she saw the prone body lying there. She had loved the old man. It was a senseless death that had come to him. Her eyes misted over with unshed tears. Then she saw Ezra's hand move ever so slowly and reach out for his gun. The tears evaporated in an instant and brought her back to the reality of what she and Josh were facing. If Ezra was alive? That meant there was a chance. A chance, perhaps, of gaining their freedom. Amy made herself concentrate. A plan of action. She had to think of some way out of this situation. Knowing Ezra was alive and armed made all the difference. There was some hope, and she had to act upon it.

"Why do you want to kill me?" Josh asked the man. Frantically thinking of ways out of their predicament, Josh had only one thought. Keep the man talking. If he kept the man talking, perhaps something would come to him. A way out might appear. Perhaps it would be only a faint chance of escape from this situation, but whilst they were still alive, he had to keep the man in conversation. Keep him talking! Josh's mind raced frantically. He asked the man again. "Why do you want to kill me? What have I ever done to hurt you? How do you know me?"

A harsh, guttural laugh came from the man. "Don't want to kill you. Nothing personal. But I do want the money I get for killing you."

"Who wants me dead? Why must I die?" Josh was

aware of the frantic note creeping into his voice and felt furious at the weakness he was betraying.

"Don't know why! I don't care either. Just know that Duke is paying me well for killing you."

"Duke who? Why does he want me dead? Why kill me?" Again, Josh's frantic voice betrayed the need to know about his past and why he was being hunted.

"Shut up! The old man is dead, and soon you'll be dead." The remark was said with a cold, bitter edge to the voice. "Then I'll have me some fun with this pretty lady. Reckon she and I will enjoy spending time together." Then came that bitter laugh. "At least I know I will!" He laughed as he pulled Amy closer to him and tightened his grip on her.

Josh knew this man would have no compunction about killing him. It meant nothing to him. It was a job, a job that obviously paid well. Was this it? Josh was not really afraid of dying, but didn't fancy it at all. What infuriated him was the fact that he might die not knowing who he was or why he was being killed.

"Yes, you'll soon be dead. But this is sure a pretty little lass. I reckon you and I can have some fun together. Plenty of places in these hills where we can have a nice, quiet time together!" Pulling Amy even closer to him, he looked her up and down and leered at her.

Amy shuddered at the closeness of the man. He laughed, enjoying her fear and dislike of him. He licked his lips, and again his eyes roved over every bit of her body. Amy squirmed away from him. "Get away from me! Leave me alone, I'll go nowhere with you!" She tried to pull away again, but his grip tightened on her. Amy spat in his face. He recoiled from her, and with the back of his hand, he wiped the spittle from his face.

"You bitch! I'll teach you some manners before I've finished breaking you in, you little hellcat." The hand holding her let go suddenly, and he backhanded her across the face with a vicious blow. She fell to the ground at his feet, and he laughed down at her. His foot drew back, and one of the ornate, black leather boots with its silver tassels kicked her in the ribs.

Josh made to dash forward, but the rifle was firmly pointed at him. His hands were clenched by his sides as he watched Amy squirm in pain. Josh moved closer and made as if to grab at the rifle. But with a sudden movement, the man twisted the rifle, grabbing it by the barrel and swiping Josh as hard as he could. Josh saw it coming and moved his head out of the way before the blow struck him. The rifle butt crashed into him just above his elbow. Josh sank to the ground in agony as the pain shot through him.

"You devil! Leave her alone. You'll pay for touching her!" Beneath his hair, which had flopped over his eyes, Josh looked at Amy. She seemed to crawl awkwardly at the man's foot. As he watched, she fumbled in one of the capacious pockets of her trousers. Amy gave a significant glance towards Josh and a slight nod. Josh didn't know what she meant to do, but he readied himself to act on whatever mad idea Amy had. He would go with it. There was nothing to lose. Any second he could be dead and then Amy... Josh wouldn't think of that, couldn't think of that!

So fast, even Josh, who was watching her, could hardly credit the speed with which Amy moved. In a single bound, she had risen, and thrust a knife deep into the man's thigh, before falling back on the ground. Blood spurted out in a gush, and he screamed and staggered back, clutching the wound.

Like a coiled spring, Josh threw himself across the intervening desert floor and flung himself at the man, attempting to grab the rifle from him. The man hit out at Josh, knocking him to the ground.

But, despite his wound, he still had hold of the rifle. By this time, the man's leg and trousers were becoming soaked with blood and he was trying to staunch the wound with one hand. All the time, he was cursing and swearing at Amy. He tried to kick out again at her, but Josh had edged forward and grabbed Amy, pulling her towards him, as far away from the man as they could scrabble.

The red bandanna was pulled from the man's neck and he tried desperately to staunch the blood, cursing all the time.

Galloping hooves came down the canyon towards them, raising clouds of dust.

# CHAPTER FIFTY-FOUR

A rider came round the corner beneath the towering rock face.

Amy's face bore the marks of the blow she had received, finger marks and a bruise already appearing. Josh found his left arm was hanging useless at his side. That blow from the rifle when he'd tried to grab it had been punishing. With his good arm, Josh pushed Amy behind him. They both were still on the floor, scrabbling about to gain purchase and trying to rise to their feet without alerting the man. Amy still had the knife in her hand. Its blade was bloodstained now. She gripped it, ready for action, and it was pointed steadily at the man, who was still trying to stop his wound from bleeding. Amy would not take another backhanded slap across her face!

The horseman was almost upon them. "It's old Gabe! What's he doing here?" Amy cried out.

The old man was shouting. "The gold is mine! All the gold belongs to me. The Thunder God has decreed that I am the one, the only one who can have the gold. Everyone has to die that tries to take my gold!" He rode nearer to them, still shouting, almost screaming at them.

The masked rider straightened up, the rifle in one hand, and his other hand still holding the bandana to his wounded thigh, attempting to staunch the blood. "Get lost, old-timer! Clear off, we don't want your gold. Get away and leave us be." The masked rider's voice was loud and clear and cut across the drumming of the galloping hooves.

Old Gabe rode on. Towards them he came, still shouting and screaming the same words again and again.

He held a huge knife in one hand. It was a large, bloodstained knife.

It was Josh who realised before the others exactly what Gabe had in his hand. His useless arm hung at his side, but with his other hand, he grabbed Amy and pulled her back towards the cliff wall of the canyon. They crouched down and scrambled further back to huddle beneath that cliff wall. Their eyes were fixed upon the old-timer, who was approaching closer and closer to them.

"Mine! The gold belongs to me. It's all mine." Gabe was almost upon the man, and his horse was galloping faster than ever.

"Look out! You're riding into me! Look out!" The masked rider screamed as the old man bore down on him.

Just as Josh thought, Gabe had no intention of riding the man down. He grabbed Amy and pulled her towards him with his good hand and thrust her face into his chest. "Don't look, Amy! Don't look!"

Mesmerised and with mounting dread, Josh's eyes focused on the scene being enacted in front of him. Gabe bent over from his horse and, with the large knife he had in his hand, he swept it across the masked rider's neck. Bile rose in Josh's throat, but somehow his willpower forced it down as he watched the head severed from the body fall and roll on the ground.

"A sacrifice for the Thunder God. The gold will always be mine!" Gabe rode around the body, but not before his eyes locked on Josh. "Death to anyone who comes near my goldmine. The Thunder God will wreak vengeance on you all." He turned his horse and Josh realised that the sight of him and Amy had provoked the old man to carry out yet more bloodshed. They were to be next!

"Come on, Amy, we need to climb up the canyon walls to get away from this madman," Josh said, pushing Amy towards the rocks.

"But what about Ezra? We can't leave him. He might be still alive. We must get to Ezra," Amy protested and pulled back from Josh's grip.

"Amy, come on! It's our only chance to escape. Gabe is turning round. He's coming back to kill us!" Josh was almost shouting at Amy. He had to get them away, out of reach of that bloodstained knife.

Gabe had turned his horse and begun heading back towards them. They were trapped against the cliff wall. The only way to escape was up, but it was a sheer rock face and gave them little chance to climb any further. Josh pushed Amy up as far as he could, trying to keep her behind him. They could only look back at the old prospector riding past Ezra, who was still lying face down on the dirt. Gabe was level with Ezra. He never gave the man a second glance. All his attention was focused on Josh and Amy. He had them in them in his sights and was determined to behead them. He began riding towards them!

# CHAPTER FIFTY-FIVE

"Take that, you murdering varmint!" A shot rang out, and they both turned round and gasped to see Ezra on his feet with his rifle aiming at Gabe. "Damn it, I missed him!" Ezra's voice held anger at his missed shot.

"Ezra is alive! Oh goodness, I'm so glad he's not dead." Amy's voice was wobbly with relief as she gazed towards the old man who stood his ground against the madman.

At the rifle shot, Gabe turned round to look at Ezra. With a regretful look at Amy and Josh, the old prospector rode back along the canyon from where he had come.

Amy tried to recover from the sight of the dead man. Amy had seen dead men before, but never had she seen such a horrible act as this. She walked away from the body and the two men standing over it. Taking deep breaths, she felt better, especially when she realised that if he had not died, she would have been his captive and Josh would be dead. Amy rejoined Ezra and Josh to stand looking down at him.

"That's the masked rider. That's the man who tried to run me down in Nowhere. It's him all right," Josh said, staring down at the man who had attempted to kill him twice.

"He said so himself, and that scarf was the one he had hiding the lower part of his face. Bright red with white spots on it, I recognised it immediately. The unusual thing about him is his boots. Remember, I threw myself on the ground in the street in Nowhere? He passed really close beside me. I saw his boots clearly. They were beside my face. I've never seen boots like that before."

Amy risked a look at the man's boots. She still had the

pain in her ribs from where one of those boots had kicked her. Ezra bent down and prodded the boot and looked at Josh. "They sure are unusual. There's fancy silver on them. No mistaking them, Josh."

"Is there anything on him which could tell you why he ran you down? And why he had to kill you?" Amy asked Josh.

Josh knelt down beside the body. It was a distasteful task, and he felt his stomach lurch constantly. Methodically, he went through each pocket of the man, frowning at the smell and touch of the bloody task. In a waistcoat pocket, Josh pulled out a small piece of paper. Sitting back on his heels, he unfolded it. The letters danced before his eyes: *Josh Barnes Broken Horseshoe Ranch.*

"What is it? What's the matter, Josh?" Amy's voice penetrated the cloud of blackness that had descended upon Josh when he read the note. Wordlessly, Josh stood up, cast a last look on the headless body, and handed Amy the paper. He walked some distance away.

Josh was aware of Amy and Ezra, reading and exclaiming over the note. Their voices drifted in and out of his consciousness as he tried to come to terms with what he had found.

A gentle touch on his arm brought him back to reality, and Amy's anxious face looked up at him. "It's the same, isn't it? The same paper and the same writing."

"Yes, almost identical. But it doesn't say '*Go to*', the other paper did." Josh knew his voice was flat, and he was finding it hard to cope with this new revelation. "What does it mean?"

"Why would someone not only want you killed, but send people after you?" Amy asked what they were all thinking.

"Yes, Josh, someone with a straightforward grudge would come up and punch you on the nose, or shoot you," puzzled Ezra.

"It must be someone with money! To pay this man would take money," Amy declared, horror-stricken at the idea. "If he can afford to send one man, you have to be on the lookout, Josh. Maybe he can afford to send others," said Amy.

"I don't know what it means, but I know what we've got to do now!" Ezra's voice called across to them. He'd led Bella towards the corpse. "Time's getting on if we're to go to Nowhere now before we get home to the ranch."

"Yes, Ezra, you're right. We've got to warn everyone about old Gabe. He's got gold fever, and it's driven him mad," Amy said and unrolled a blanket from Bella's back.

"Let me help you, Ezra. After all, I've done it before." Josh said these words with a grimace, but he placed, with Ezra's help, the corpse on poor Bella's back in a matter of minutes, despite his damaged arm.

Before mounting their horses, Josh turned to speak to them. "I don't want this note mentioned to anyone else except those at the ranch. Someone wants me dead. I'd rather they didn't know I knew about it. Let them think I'm still ignorant of their plans."

It was decided that Ezra was riding the man's horse, Josh was on Ezra's horse, and Amy was on her usual one. Bella, of course, had the body.

They rode together in a sombre silence. There was nothing to say: not about the dead man, or about Gabe. It was a collection of questions with no answers, and nothing they could think or say would bring forward any answers. So many questions! When would they get answers?

# CHAPTER FIFTY-SIX

It took Amy some time to recover from the sight of the death of the masked man. It was Ezra and Josh who had placed the dead body over Bella. This time, Bella didn't even bother looking to see the burden. The head also joined Bella's baggage.

It was Ezra who had survived unscathed. The bullet had whistled past his ear, and he flung himself off his horse to pretend to be dead, hoping that no more shots would be fired at him. It had worked, and he had lain there waiting for an opportunity to rescue the others. It was with difficulty that he had watched Amy being ill-treated, but he realised that there was nothing he could do at that time.

"I really thought Gabe was about to slice all our heads off as well. Those shots of yours, Ezra, saved us. He didn't like you shooting at him. Probably thought three of us were too many for him to tackle," Josh said as he struggled to ride on the horse with only one arm in full use.

"Are you all right, Amy? Are you fit enough to ride back to Nowhere?" Josh looked closely at the girl, aching to give her a hug. She was so white and her freckles stood out like vivid spots against the pallor of her complexion.

"Yes, Josh, I'm okay. What about you? That injured arm looks serious. Will you manage to ride back with only one arm in full use?"

"You've both got to ride to Nowhere with me. Stop asking each other if you're all right. You've got to be! Let's get going. Time is a-wasting. We got to get to Nowhere and get some men out after that madman before he kills again." Ezra's voice made them both laugh at each other, and without another word they rode their horses back to Nowhere with another dead, headless man. This time, they did have his head in a bag!

The terrain was rocky with gravelly patches. Straggling, stunted trees grew in twisted shapes, the hot wind and the baking sun contorting their branches. Cacti were everywhere, spines of different lengths and varying poisonous effects were ready to snag an unwary traveller.

Although late in the afternoon, the sun had lost little of its ferocious power. All three of them were soon exhausted and sweating. Riding down narrow gullies and wandering round behind giant cacti was a difficult and unrewarding task. But they knew they had to make the fastest time they could to get back to Nowhere. They rode close to each other, taking some comfort in each other's presence. But not one of them spoke. What could be said? They had survived a terrible ordeal and were all still trying to come to terms with it.

Late afternoon sun streamed across the main street in Nowhere. They were weary after this enforced detour to that day's gold treasure prospecting, and they rode in silence to the sheriff's office. It was Ezra who jumped down and shouted for the Preacher. By this time, there were a few horrified townspeople following in their wake.

"It's another body!"

"They've got another headless corpse!"

"Where are they getting these bodies? And who's killing everyone?"

The questions came at once and altogether. The trio ignored them: too tired and worn out to waste energy on replies.

"Where's the head? Have they got the head this time?"

A man shouted from the back of the crowd.

Emerging from his office, still wearing his long black coat despite the heat of the day, the Preacher stopped in astonishment. "You again! And with another headless body?"

"Not headless this time. We have the head. It was old Gabe who did it. We saw him with a large knife. He rode past the man and slashed his head clean off. He's the one that's been chopping everybody's heads off. The old man has gone raving mad," Ezra said as he dismounted.

The Preacher walked over to the body. "Do you know who he is? Any idea?"

"He was here yesterday, rode wildly down the street. He nearly rode me over, but we don't know who he is. Maybe somebody else spoke to him yesterday," Josh said, and looked around at the growing crowd.

"I see that red spotted scarf. The guy wearing that came into the saloon yesterday and brought a drink," the saloon owner said to both Josh and Amy as they also dismounted. "He was in here asking about Broken Horseshoe Ranch. Where was it? And who lived there? Pointed out Josh, I did, told him he was the nephew of the sick guy that lives there. Drank his drink down and was gone."

All eyes switched from the saloonkeeper to Josh. It was Eliza who spoke up, deflecting all the interest in Josh. She and Manuel from the general store had come to see what was going on with the crowd around the sheriff's office.

"Come on, Sheriff Preacher, get this body ready for a Christian burial. Let those horses be fed and watered, and I'll take these folks to my place for a wash and a bite to eat."

The Preacher reluctantly had to agree. Eliza was in the right of it and he began shouting out orders. "We need to find Gabe. Track him down and stop him from killing anyone else," said the Preacher. "We must find Gabe!"

# CHAPTER FIFTY-SEVEN

"I suggest we go back to where Gabe beheaded that man and track Gabe from there. Who's a good tracker? Anyone here?" said Manuel.

"I'll find him for you." A tall Indian stepped forward. Nothing on him told of which tribe he belonged to. He wore buckskin trousers and a cotton shirt, and had a gun holster, and a knife also on him. Tall and muscular, he towered over some of the smaller men beside him.

Dark-skinned, there was little to point him out as an Indian. It was more his surrounding aura that proclaimed his ethnicity. His long hair was pulled back from his face and tied at the neck. Dark eyes were set in a chiselled, handsome face with high cheekbones and narrow lips.

"Oh, Sam, you're the very man for the task. You work in the livery stable, don't you? Okay, you saddle up. Everyone else join us at the general store, and we'll set out and catch Gabe." The Preacher gave the orders and watched as the men rushed off. They were eager not only for vengeance but intent on halting old Gabe's deadly obsession with his mine and his love of gold.

"Josh, are you fit enough to show me where you last saw Gabe?" the Preacher said to Josh, who was standing beside him.

"Yes, Preacher, my arm will be fine till we get back. Someone can attend to it then. I'll show you where Gabe was last seen," answered Josh.

"I'll go too," Ezra and Amy both said in unison. There was no stopping either of them.

"I want him caught. That man can't be left alone out there a moment longer. And I know that part of the country better than any one of you!" Ezra said, his long white hair bobbing up and down in time with his agitated remarks as he showed his determination to be one of the posse. "I missed him once, I won't miss him a second time!" Ezra vowed, his lined face angry that the chance he'd had of killing the man had slipped through his fingers.

"Not you, Amy. It's no place for a woman in a posse chasing a murderer. You'd be no help at all. You'd just be a hindrance." Eliza had come up to stand behind Amy. She knew the girl would be keen to chase after Gabe, but she realised Amy was exhausted. Eliza had often heard tales of the action that had taken place on the hunt for a murderer. That was no place for Amy.

Eliza and Amy stood on the boardwalk with the others. The posse was gathering outside the general store. They were milling about, discussing the terrible events that had been taking place. The horses were restless, and the men were eager to get off. Each one of them had a burning resolve to get old Gabe and end his reign of terror.

"No one's safe while he's roaming around. He's not only going for anyone who might attack him or who will steal gold from his mine, he's going for anyone he can see. It doesn't matter what they're doing out in the mountains, he's killing and beheading every single person he sees," cried out one man.

"We'll get him!" shouted another man.

"Sure will!" some others chimed in together.

The large, black horse that the Preacher rode came galloping out of the livery stable. His black coat tails were flying out behind him like bat wings. "Are you all ready? Let's go!" he shouted at the men as he came up to them, his horse prancing in excitement.

With a chorus of shouts and hurrahs, the assembled

crowd galloped off behind the Preacher, eager to stop Gabe and his murdering ways.

"I should have gone with them!" Amy said. She stood outside the general store with both hands on the hitching rail, watching the cloud of dust as the posse charged off towards the mountains. "I could have..."

"Nonsense! A posse is no place for a young girl. I've told you already, a girl doesn't go on a search for a murderer. You've had enough trouble and excitement for this day. Look at you. Just look at the state of you, Amy Tanner!" Eliza stood in front of Amy, her hands planted on her hips, a mock angry expression on her face.

"But I..." Amy tried to speak again.

This time, Eliza placed a finger on her lips. "You can't go home to your Pa in that state. Come on, look at you." Pushing Amy in front of her, she took the girl to a curtain at the back of the shop. This was Eliza's new idea. A large, broken mirror from a wardrobe was leaning up against the wall, and there were piles of clothes and rows of material stacked neatly in place beside it. Taking Amy's arm, Eliza pushed her in front of the mirror.

Amy stared into the mirror. Her braids had come undone, and her hair hung loose in tangles down her back. The bruised face with a quickly blackening eye was smeared with dust and dirt. Her canvas skirt was torn up the side, not only from where she'd been thrown to the ground by the masked rider, but also where she'd struggled to get her knife out. Amy hadn't realised that she'd sliced part of her skirt and was appalled at how she looked. She could hardly recognise herself, so dirty and dishevelled she had become. Amy agreed with Eliza that she had become a terrible mess.

Aware of the older woman rummaging amongst the

clothes beside her, Amy turned round to watch her.

"This one!" Eliza said triumphantly.

Amy's eyes widened as Eliza held up a dark tan skirt and a pretty blue blouse before her. "Your size! Go out to the back and wash up. Then fix your hair and put these clothes on and we'll get you something to eat and drink. Amy, go on! I've already sent Ramon to tell your Pa you are staying with me for the night after the nasty experience you've gone through. Amy, go!"

# CHAPTER FIFTY-EIGHT

The order said with a smile by Eliza made Amy laugh, and she did as she was told. Not a vain girl, Amy thought little of her appearance as a rule. Her hair was always neat and tidy, her clothes washed and serviceable, and that was her ready to face the world.

But today, when she tucked the blouse into the new skirt, Amy had a desire to see exactly what she looked like in these new clothes. Eliza had even given her matching blue ribbons to tie up her braids. Amy crept out to the back of the store and went behind the curtain. She looked at the young woman who stared back at her. Neat and tidy had been what she had expected. Amy received a shock at the reflection of the young woman who looked back at her. The soft blue of the blouse, which had pretty lace edging round the collar, made her hair's auburn tints shine in the neatly plaited braids that fell down to her waist. Smoothing the skirt, its shape and style were much more feminine and stylish compared to the canvas skirts and trousers Amy was usually dressed in. Amy smiled. The thought crept into her mind, and she wondered if Josh would like how she looked. Flushing, she turned away from the mirror to join Eliza in her kitchen. But not before she had another last look.

Amy felt strange in her new outfit, but excited at how it made her feel feminine and yet was practical at the same time. "I love these clothes, Eliza, but I must pay you for them," Amy said as she walked from behind the curtain to join the other woman. But it was with a heavy heart that she joined Eliza. There was little enough money for food and her father's occasional treats these days. New clothes for her were a luxury, but somehow she vowed they would be paid for. She would not give them back! She loved them and how she looked in them was amazing.

"I'd rather you didn't pay me for them," Eliza said with a hopeful look at Amy.

"What do you mean, Eliza?" Amy asked and looked at the older woman.

Eliza sat down on a wooden, roughhewn chair that they always kept at the counter. The few women that lived in the township liked to sit for a while when they shopped. A visit to the general store was not something to be hurried. Sitting for a time meant that whatever news or gossip of the day could be discussed and exclaimed over at length. Some women made it a weekly outing along with the Sunday service. But several of the women would not attend the Preacher's Sunday services. He conducted them in the saloon, and a glass of whiskey or beer could be seen in many of the congregation members' hands, including the Preacher himself! Immediately after the service was over, the usual rowdy atmosphere renewed itself with an increased vigour.

"Sit down, Amy, and join me. You see, my dear, it's like this, I'm pregnant again."

Eliza waved away Amy's murmured congratulations and began speaking again. "Last time I was expecting a baby, I was ill most of the time. I'm a lot older now, and I have to take greater care of myself. Manuel does all the heavy work, as you know. But part of the time he delivers to other ranches and brings back produce for the store."

Amy nodded at this speech of Eliza's but was wondering where it was going and if she would ever get there.

"I know Nancy is out at your ranch most days. So I

wondered if you could spare the time now to come and work here for a couple of days a week. Manuel could use those days for all his deliveries. When he's away from the general store, he'd be happier knowing that you were with me."

Amy looked around the store. Manuel had laid a wooden floor, and built counters to store goods below, with goods piled above on shelves. There was coffee, tea, and a variety of food items, including hams, bacon, barrels of flour, meal, vinegar, and salt pork. Crocks of honey and baskets of eggs were all muddled up with peppermint candy sticks and horehound candy drops. On one side of the store, there was a variety of goods, including dishes, pails, shovels, and brooms. A lot of the products on sale had been brought in by ranchers in return for merchandise. Amy realised that the eggs and the pork and other goods like that must have been bartered by Manuel on his day trips. The store was interesting. Well, to Amy, it was fascinating, and she knew she would love to work in it. But there was one thought at the front of her mind and that was frightening. Staring fixedly at Eliza, Amy blurted it out. "What if the baby comes?"

Eliza went off into peals of laughter. "Bless you, child, it's months away! There are other women in the township I can call on for that sort of help."

"Yes, then, I'd love to help you out," Amy said with no hesitation now.

"You haven't asked what your wages would be?" Eliza said to the girl.

"Wages?" said Amy, embarrassed at the very thought.

"Manuel and I talked it over between us. We'd work it out in goods and provisions each week. How would that be?"

Amy thought that would be great and looked forward to her first day at work. "These clothes I am wearing?"

"Those you are going to earn right now. Manuel has gone off with the posse and you'll have to help me close up the store for the night."

"Do you think they will catch him? Old Gabe will fight. I hope no one gets hurt," Amy said as she helped Eliza close the double doors of the general store.

Both women looked out at the darkness that had descended over the small township of Nowhere. Eliza closed the door and shot the bolt, then whispered softly. "Yes, let's hope nobody gets hurt."

# CHAPTER FIFTY-NINE

The mixed assortment of men who straggled out of the town of Nowhere were united in one purpose, and that was to rid the world of old Gabe. The once harmless character that had been Gabe, the old gold prospector, was now a deadly menace to all those who travelled in the area around Nowhere and the Devil's Mountain. Unpredictable and somehow gaining the upper hand of each victim, he displayed a callous disregard for his victims. Beheaded, their bodies lay where they had fallen, but their heads were never found near them. Where were their heads? Had Gabe taken them away with him? Where had he taken them? And why?

Talk between the men had ceased. The determination with which they had set out on their quest had not diminished. But the heat of the day had not lessened as the afternoon wore on. The heat, and the horror and bloodshed that they may have to face, had caused the tongues to still.

That pleased Josh. Questions had been flung at him, comments made which required answers. Polite answers! Josh really wanted to tell them to leave him alone. The day had held too much for him already. He was finding it hard to absorb and process what had already happened to him. His mind shrieked at him as the pain in his arm increased with every jolt of his horse. Josh felt at breaking point and kept quiet and apart from the others.

Reaching the scene of the masked rider's death brought each one of the men in the posse to the realisation of how evil the man they sought was. The bloodstained ground was a mute witness to the macabre event that had happened earlier. Josh, who had lived through it, found on his return that it affected him even more. He could see the action Gabe had produced with the knife. It replayed again and again in his mind. Josh found it hard to stop the bile that rose in his throat yet again and swallowed hard.

Sam took the lead and followed the tracks Gabe had made. At first, it was easy to trace the passage of the old prospector. The afternoon was drawing in and shadows were appearing: the stick-like figures from the saguaro cacti, and the lengthening shapes from the boulders, rocks, and the canyon walls. It had been decided to carry on searching for Gabe. There was going to be a full moon that night, and it was easier at times to search in the cool of the evening.

An undercurrent of excitement ran through the men as they continued further into the mountains after Gabe. On the ridge they had been climbing up, Sam raised a hand. "Quiet now. We're getting closer to his lair."

The last part of the climb wasn't steep at all, but it was arduous because they had to guide the horses around many boulders. Sam's hand gestured again, and he dismounted, tying his horse to a scrubby tree. The others followed him, and without their horses and keeping as quiet as possible, they joined him as he stood silently on the crest of the ridge.

Below them, a stone building, small and tumbledown, was set on a patch of scrubby grass: a tiny valley in the midst of all the mountain peaks.

"That was an old-timer's mine, and a store for the miners. Look at all the scattered debris around it," whispered Ezra in Josh's ear. The detritus of an early mining venture lay, with old, rusty metal implements and broken old tools, scattered about amongst weeds and tall grasses. A fire was built up before the open door of the square building. At the back of the building, two mules and a horse were tethered on a patch of grass and beneath a couple of trees. There was no one to be seen.

Sam stood silent, very much the Indian, with his impassive face, noble bearing, and chiselled features.

"Do we rush him?" whispered the blacksmith.

"No, wait," was Sam's whispered reply.

Silhouetted against the flames of the fire, Gabe came out of the building. Oblivious to them watching, he threw more fuel on the fire and began dancing around it. A wild laugh escaped from his lips, then he started shouting out loud. "Mine! All the gold belongs to me. The Thunder God says kill them all."

"I'll retrieve the horse and the mules. We don't want him escaping on them," Sam said.

"Take me with you. It'll be easier with the two of us," said Josh. He looked at the other men in the posse, who were citizens of Nowhere, which was a frontier group of shops and houses, too small to be called a town proper. But it was trying hard to be a prosperous frontier town. Hardened men they may have been, and living a tough life in ranches, shops, and in Nowhere itself. But some were overweight or getting on in years, and not one of them was as fit as he was to go down with Sam and retrieve the old prospector's horses.

"Very well. How will we know it's safe to come down and capture him?" the Preacher said.

"He's got some kettle or pot on the edge of the fire. I'll shoot at that. When he looks at it, he won't see you arriving, because his eyes will have been looking into the fire."

"We'll wait for the signal," replied the Preacher.

# CHAPTER SIXTY

Shadow-like, Sam disappeared into the approaching evening darkness. Blinking at first, unable to see him, Josh walked behind him, finding the path easier than he expected as he followed the Indian.

Sam paused for a moment, checking on the position of Gabe.

Josh tapped him on the shoulder. "Thought you should know, that masked rider banged up my arm, and it's pretty useless."

Reaching forward, Sam grabbed Josh's arm and began kneading it with his fingers. Josh bit his lip so hard he could taste the blood. He had to, otherwise he'd have screamed at the excruciating pain. The Indian gave Josh a wry smile, almost revelling in the pain he was causing. Then Sam stepped back. Josh's arm was on fire, the heat throbbing in wave after wave. Then it was gone. Josh moved his arm, tentatively at first, then with an easier pain-free movement.

At Josh's obvious delight at his almost pain-free arm, Sam gave him a grin, and moved forward again. Slowly, they edged towards the animals and, untying them one at a time, began leading them well away from Gabe and the building. Tethering them, they crept back again. Gabe was busy feeding the fire. Bending over a kettle, he sat on a stool beside it.

"I'll hit the kettle. You aim for the middle of the fire. That should make it flare up and startle the man. It will give the Preacher the signal," Sam whispered to Josh.

Josh took out his gun and aimed at the centre of the fire. At a nod from Sam, he fired.

The kettle took the brunt of it. The loud noise of

bullets hitting metal made everyone jump. Gabe leapt off the stool, out of the way of the splashing water. The gunshots from Josh sent sparks and broken fiery twigs shooting up into the night sky. This latest assault upon his fire had Gabe jumping again and staggering backwards. The hissing of steam erupting as it hit the ground and the sparks flying into the air combined with the shouts of Gabe. It was a tremendous noise which shattered the mountain stillness of the night.

"Now! " The Preacher's voice rang out into the darkness and was followed by the shouts and whoops of the men charging down the hillside. "Stand still, Gabe. Put your hands in the air! You are surrounded!" The Preacher's voice, used to sermonising loud and long, rang out, bouncing around the rocky cliff walls that enclosed the tiny valley. Descending to the valley floor with galumphing strides, his large coat with its billowing coattails, he appeared like an Old Testament prophet, bringing death and destruction in retribution for Gabe's evil deeds.

Gabe made to run to his horse but was met by the two figures of Sam and Josh, guns pointing straight at him. Whirling around, the old man started screaming. "Thunder God, where are you? Save me from these men. Thunder God, where are you?" Realisation hit the old man at the sight of the approaching men with their guns drawn. Their set, determined faces of horror at his actions made him throw up his hands and he crumpled onto the ground and began sobbing.

"Tie him up and put him on one of his mules ready to go back to Nowhere, and to gaol." The Preacher gave out the order and began looking around the camp that Gabe had used for such a long time.

"Preacher, come and see this! It's all the heads!" The cry came from inside the stone building. "There are seven of them, all on the shelf."

Never did any of the men wish to talk about the experience they endured. They took the heads from the building, having previously dug a long grave. All the heads were placed within it. The ground covered them up and large stones placed on top.

"This is a task I never dreamt I would have to perform. A task horrific in its nature by a man steeped in evil." The Preacher paused for a moment, finding it difficult to put into words what he and all the others were feeling. He said prayers over the dead men's heads.

All stood in respectful silence around that sad grave. Josh felt the pressure of the mountains as they overhung that tiny valley. Flickering firelight threw the faces of the surrounding men into sharp relief. Some were sad-faced and prayed earnestly. Other faces bore witness to the horror they had seen. It was etched in harsh lines on their faces. A constant muttering from old Gabe was in the background of the Preacher's words. As the Preacher finished speaking, shuffling feet, coughs, and clearing of throats accompanied that last "Amen."

After that, they got ready to leave the sad, desolate place. The men had scattered, searching around the building, and amongst the few scrappy possessions of Gabe.

"Look at this! There's piles of rock here, all sorted into different shapes and sizes. But they're ordinary rocks, they're not gold at all." The man lifted a couple of the larger rocks, one in each hand, to show the others. "Do you think Gabe thought...?"

# CHAPTER SIXTY-ONE

At the sight of the man holding these two rocks, Gabe began screaming and flung himself off the mule. "That's my gold! Leave my gold alone. The Thunder God gave it to me!"

The Preacher had had enough. With his enormous strength, he lifted the man and was about to slap him across the face when he stopped. Looking up towards heaven, he said, "Okay Lord, anyone got a scarf? We can gag this fellow then."

The journey back to Nowhere was almost an anticlimax. Dusk had fallen, and as it grew dark, the moon lit up the route back, almost as bright as daylight. The posse returning to Nowhere had achieved its aim of catching the murderer. But a lingering sadness crept over every one of them as they realised that the men who had been beheaded had been done so for ordinary rocks.

Outside the sheriff's office, a crowd had gathered, and the horror of their discovery of the heads was told, again and again. A struggling Gabe was taken into the sheriff's office and put into a cell. The gag was removed from his mouth, and the constant muttering and screaming began from him. The Preacher shut the door on him and came out to the crowd gathered in front of the office. "Go home. We've caught the murderer, buried the bodies and the heads. There's nothing more to see here. Let's get some rest. Gabe will have to be taken for trial tomorrow. For goodness' sake, people, go home. Let's all have some rest!"

Ezra took Josh to one side. "Amy is exhausted and should stay the night with Eliza. With your arm, you are in no fit state to ride back to the ranch. I'll tell them what's happened. Now both killers are dead. I should be safe enough on the journey," Ezra said.

"Are you sure, Ezra? It would certainly put Luke and Nancy's minds at rest." Josh watched as the old man rode off to the ranch. Then Josh took his horse to the livery stable. The excitement around the sheriff's office at the arrival of the posse and old Gabe was too much for him. It was too noisy. After the experiences of the day, all Josh craved was silence, to get his muddled thoughts in some sort of order. On reaching the stable, he found Sam tending to the needs of each horse that had been dropped off earlier.

"Thank you, Sam. Your magic trick with my arm worked wonders. It's still painful, but not nearly so bad, and I can move it around."

"No magic, just old-fashioned Indian medical know-how," was Sam's reply. He came forward to take Josh's horse from him and smiled at Josh.

"I'll do my horse, thanks. You've got enough to do by the look of it." Josh gestured to a couple more horses waiting their turn to be attended to. "Medical know-how? Seems to me you are too highly qualified to be working in a livery stable." Josh paused as he walked forward with his horse into the stable proper. He looked at Sam, really looked at Sam, as if it was for the first time. What was the difference in him? He was no longer the slouching, self-effacing Indian tracker that had joined the posse. During that time, Sam had done his job, and the only people he had spoken to were the Preacher and Josh himself. Now, the Indian stood tall and straight and looked Josh in the eye, no longer looking down at the ground or sliding his eyes away. He was the Indian who had saved them from Sheriff Cody!

Sam grinned at Josh's intense stare. The Indian realised what Josh was thinking and found it amusing. "With you, Josh, I don't need to be the stereotypical Indian," Sam said.

"Whoa! Medical knowledge and words like stereotypical! Wait a minute! Who are you, Sam? Where did you, supposedly lowly plains Indian, learn words like that? And what's more, learn how and when to use them?"

Sam laughed. It was the first laugh that Josh had ever heard from him. It changed his face and bearing in an instant. This smiling, cheerful Indian, Josh felt, was a revelation.

"Someday, Josh, I will tell you my story. I think you and I both have strange backgrounds and that life for both of us has been out of the ordinary. But not now. That will be for another time."

Josh had finished with his horse and patted it as he watched it feed. He turned back towards the Indian who was dealing with another horse. "Alright, Sam, but I'll hold you to that! I'm determined to find out how you come to be educated, not only in the basics but to such a high standard. I would tell you my life story, but I don't know what it is. Keep this to yourself please, but I had a blow on the head, and have lost my memory because of it."

"That is intriguing," the Indian said as he finished one horse and moved on to the second horse. He lifted his head, and they both turned at the sound of approaching voices. Moving closer to Josh, Sam whispered to him. "I need your help. Your people at Broken Horseshoe Ranch are the only ones I can rely on and trust. Can I come out to the ranch and speak with you all?"

"Of course, Sam. You saved all our lives. We are in your debt. Can you doubt we would help you? When will you come?"

"I'm uncertain which night it will be. But soon, listen out for me. I'll give you a signal."

"We'll be ready and waiting for you," Josh said.

The Indian dropped his voice even further and moved closer to Josh. "Have you heard of Shadowhawk?" He stared at Josh intently, looking for a sign of recognition at the name.

"No. Who is he?" Josh asked. "Who is Shadowhawk?"

# CHAPTER SIXTY-TWO

On the arrival of several men all talking at once, Sam reverted to his inconspicuous Indian persona and went back to tending the horses. A curious glance at Sam gave no clue to Josh what was worrying Sam. Realising the opportunity to talk had gone, Josh left the livery stable and walked back down towards the general store.

Josh opened the back door of the general store to be greeted by Manuel, placing a beer into his hand. Manuel had already returned before him and had told the women all about the capture of Gabe and the finding and burial of the severed heads. "Take it! I'm on my second one. You need it after the day you've had."

A swallow, and then another one, and Josh felt slightly better. It had been a tough day to say the least, but the beer helped. Josh was not a drinker, and only occasionally drank a beer or a whiskey, but he felt today he had earned it.

"Come on in. Eliza is going to dish up supper for us. I've been telling them all about Gabe."

Already seated at the table were Ramon and Amy. Both looked up at him and smiled. Manuel settled himself at the head of the table, whilst Eliza busied herself at the stove. Amy got up and handed out the filled plates piled high with roast pork and vegetables. She and Eliza worked together as a team. Josh noted how comfortable Amy was with the Mexican woman. He also noted a difference in the young woman. Yes, Amy really was a young woman. To his puzzled eyes, he wondered why Amy no longer looked like a girl anymore. Why was that? Josh wondered. Then he took a closer look. No longer clad in the worn canvas trousers or faded checked shirt, Amy was now dressed in new clothes: an outfit that showed she was a girl no more. Amy was a young woman now, and a very desirable one at that. Suddenly conscious that he was staring at her, he blurted out before he could stop himself. "You look pretty in your new clothes, Amy."

It had been the right thing to do. Amy blushed with pleasure, and Eliza gave him an approving nod.

"Did you see the state of the clothes she was wearing? Torn and filthy from the rough manhandling she got from that beast," Eliza said, plonking a dish of green beans down on the table with unnecessary force at the thought of the beast.

The plates were all handed out, the vegetables in their bowls put on the table, and bread sliced up, ready for dipping in the gravy. There was silence while they ate their meal.

"Why didn't you eat your meal earlier?" Manuel asked Eliza through a mouthful of roast pork.

"We couldn't face eating the meal then. We were so worried about what was happening to you all that we just didn't feel like it," Eliza said.

"But there were many of us, and Gabe was only one man," protested Manuel. "You should have eaten, especially now."

Josh looked puzzled at this remark and Eliza explained it to him. "I'm expecting a baby, Josh, and as I'm a lot older now, Manuel worries about me," laughed Eliza.

"And I'm going to help at the general store, two days a week. It will be money for the ranch. That's if Pa will let me," Amy told him with a mounting excitement in her voice. "Do you think Pa will agree to it?" Her face clouded over at the thought that he might refuse.

"Yes, I'm sure he will," Josh said, delighted at this fresh interest in Amy's dull life. "Perhaps you could find me a job, too, Manuel?" he joked.

An exchange of looks between husband and wife showed a previous conversation between them had taken place. Manuel began speaking. "Well, Josh, Eliza and I have been thinking..."

Shouts interrupted Manuel. "Fire! Fire! The sheriff's office is on fire!"

# CHAPTER SIXTY-THREE

As one, they rose to their feet and rushed to the front of the general store. Josh was thankful he had finished his meal. He had been enjoying it so much. Further dramatic events needed to be faced on a full stomach, was the ridiculous thought he had, as he, too, rushed out to see what was happening. When they emerged from the general store, it was to find others were already running down the street.

"Bucket chain! Bucket chain!" The Preacher's voice roared above the crowd and the crackling fire. Men ran to get buckets and fill them from the water at the livery stable. In seconds, a chain of them were passing buckets of water from one to the other.

"It's useless. The fire has taken hold already. There's no way buckets of water will put that out," the Preacher said, his long, thin face clouded with anger.

The door of the office was open, and a man was pushing Gabe out through the door. Flames were licking at their feet and rising to the roof behind them. "Get out, man! Get out, Gabe!" Two other men dropped their buckets and rushed towards the deputy and Gabe, pulling them to safety out onto the road. When they reached the roadway and safety, they turned to look back at the office, where beams in the roof were now ablaze.

"That was a newly built office. Only decent building in the town, and now look at it!" The Preacher's voice rang out yet again. "Save the water, lads, it's no good. Fire's got such a hold on it now. We'll have to let it burn itself out."

"The Thunder God's calling me. The fire is mine. It's for me!" Gabe shook himself loose from the man who was holding his arm and ran straight back into the building. A couple of men made as if to stop him.

"Let him be! Don't anyone risk their lives for that man!" shouted the Preacher.

His deputy shouted across the crowd at the Preacher. "It's what he wants, all right! Who do you think set the fire? It was well alight in his cell before I realised what he had done. Somehow, Gabe set the fire himself."

There were horrified gasps and shrieks from some women as all eyes went to the figure of Gabe. He could be seen capering about in the middle of the burning building. His figure was silhouetted against the fiery flames. Then, with a crash, the roof caved in. Gabe disappeared in a roar of flames, crashes of falling timbers, and showers of sparks.

Next morning, Amy was hugged by Eliza as they stood outside the general store. Josh shook his good hand with those of Manuel and the Preacher. They were on their way back to Broken Horseshoe Ranch. The Preacher had joined them in the store where he was getting provisions. He now wished Amy and Josh well on their journey back to the ranch.

Amy smiled at Eliza, who had whispered in her ear how pretty she looked in her new clothes. "Thank you so much. I'll see you on my first day of work." Amy felt such a warmth for the Mexican couple. They had welcomed her and Josh and made them feel part of their family.

"I wonder what Nancy will have done to the ranch in your absence?" Eliza said with a laugh.

"Something! She won't have been sitting still, of that I'm certain," said Amy and joined in with Eliza's laughter.

No longer did she dread Nancy upsetting the routine that she and her brother and father had enjoyed. That was then. Fresh changes were happening, whether or not Amy wanted them. Amy smiled and looked at her friend. "Do you know it's always interesting when we return home? In fact, if nothing outrageously different has happened up at Broken Horseshoe Ranch, I'll be disappointed!"

Both women laughed, and Amy got on her horse. Josh stood beside her. "Okay, Amy, have you got everything?"

"You mean, Josh, have I remembered to pack the apple pie Eliza made for you? It's in my saddlebag here." Amy patted the bag behind her.

As they were talking, Sam approached them. They were out of earshot of anyone else. Sam came closer. "Miss Amy, here's your new gun holster." He handed Amy a beautifully worked leather holster.

"But Sam, I never..."

"Hush, Amy. No one must hear this. Watch out for Shadowhawk! Have extra men on guard each night. That's when he comes." Sam drifted away, leaving Amy looking down at the beautifully wrought gun holster. Josh looked at her with meaning. They would talk later, that look meant. Amy nodded in agreement.

Waving goodbye to their friends as they set off home produced mixed feelings. Both Josh and Amy had enjoyed their visit with the Mexican couple, and both were looking forward to working at the store alongside them. They had also the overwhelming relief at the death of Gabe. It meant the end of his killing spree. They were silent as they rode back home to Broken Horseshoe Ranch. Thoughts of the cryptic comments from Sam about Shadowhawk mingled with the frightening puzzle of who was out to kill Josh.

They would be home at lunchtime. They had quite a story to tell and explain to the others. Perhaps Nancy had some other unexpected plan for the ranch, and Leah would produce a wonderful meal for them.

"We have a lot to tell them about, haven't we, Amy?" Josh said as the ranch came into view.

"Yes, Josh. It's going to take some telling! But it's good to be home."

A smile passed between them as they heard Ben's voice. "They're coming! Amy and Josh are coming."

They could see Ben waving, Chan waving, and even Luke and Nancy had joined in the greetings from the porch.

They rode under the Broken Horseshoe Ranch sign and Josh turned to Amy with a puzzled expression on his face. "Who's Shadowhawk?" Josh asked Amy.

"I don't know, I've never heard the name before," was her reply.

The warning words of Sam lingered in their minds as they approached the ranch. "Watch out for Shadowhawk!"

## About The Author

Janey Clarke writes charming, witty, cozy mysteries. From septuagenarian shenanigans in Cornwall to the intrigue of Regency-era whodunits and now to her newest venture into the rugged drama of the Wild West. When not plotting her next twist or researching historical details, she can be found exploring the stunning Jurassic Coast in Dorset with her loyal spaniel by her side. With a passion for tea, old books, and well-timed humour, Janey Clarke creates stories she hopes will whisk readers away to delightful worlds where solving a mystery is always the order of the day. And always solved by a feisty heroine! Visit her at www.janeyclarke.com to learn more about her books.

# Acknowledgements.

For my son Iain, whose unwavering support and encouragement has kept me going on this writing journey.

Sharon Garles, thank you for your enthusiasm for my Devil's Mountain characters!

www.blossomspringpublishing.com